The Adventures of the G.C. Boys:

The Cure for Death

By Ian Ramos

AmErica House
Baltimore

Copyright 2001 by Ian Ramos.
All rights reserved. No part of this book may be reproduced in any form without written permission from the publishers, except by a reviewer who may quote brief passages in a review to be printed in a newspaper or magazine.

First printing

ISBN: 1-58851-040-9
PUBLISHED BY AMERICA HOUSE BOOK PUBLISHERS
www.publishamerica.com
Baltimore

Printed in the United States of America

Dedicated
To
Cynthia McDaniel Ramos

Chapter 1

The Jeepman

A bead of sweat rolled down my forehead. It brushed against my eyebrow and then plummeted to the pillow below. I sunk my teeth into my lower lip, hoping the pain would bring me to consciousness. The self-inflicted discomfort did not accomplish its feat, for I still tossed and turned in my bed, separating my sheets from my blankets as drops of perspiration continuously rolled down my forehead into my pillow. I quivered in fear, as my mind tried to regain control of its thoughts.

The dreams had surfaced over a year ago. The nightmares came infrequently, bearing messages that foretold my eventual doom. But this past month, the apparitions had gone out of control. Nightmarish visions now haunted me on a weekly basis. The dreams were almost indistinguishable. My mind kept replaying the same image of me lying down in some kind of wooden box. From previous dreams, I now knew the box to be a coffin. I would find myself again each night wearing the same navy blue suit with the same plaid necktie. I would be lying face up in the frigid wooden box that had its interior lined with maroon velvet carpeting.

This morbid case was awkward and uncomfortable and left me little room for movement. I pushed the top of the box trying to open it, yet the top would not move. I tried again, this time pushing with all my strength. This time, the top started to budge slightly. Grains of sand began to seep in from the sides as the lid moved further. Then suddenly, the roof of the coffin collapsed inward as a mountain of sand poured upon me. I quickly sat up in my bed as the image vanished from my mind.

"I don't want to die," I kept thinking to myself as I sat up in my bed, panting heavily. I had lived my entire life thinking I would live forever, and now at the age of fourteen it seemed I had, for some unknown reason, discovered my mortality. I was now scared of aging. I was terrified of growing up, for I knew they both would bring about my demise. Of all my fears, what frightened me the most was that I knew that there was no way I could halt death, for Lady Death was a natural part of life. Death was as important to the circle of life as was being born.

    I began brainstorming, trying frantically to come up with some way that I could stop death. I was an extremely creative boy. I had solved over seventy percent of the video games that had crossed my path - I could decipher this morbid riddle. After hours of rummaging through my mind, an idea leaped into my head. Earlier this year, I had read of a Spanish explorer who searched the Florida Keys for a fountain of youth. A sip of this water would keep you eternally young, and as I replayed the legend in my head, the pieces of the puzzle began to fit into place. Suddenly, it all made sense. "I won't die," I told myself. "I won't die."

    The idea seemed rather simplistic; the logic made perfect sense. If I stayed a kid, then I could not age, and if I could not age, then I could not die. Death would never lay its fingers upon me. Death would never take me into its abode. As the idea stewed in my head, I smiled, as it would bring about other benefits. I would never have to deal with paying bills, getting married, or having a job. I would never own a face filled with wrinkles, or have a mid-life crisis, and I would never obtain some withered, old body. It would be like I was some sort of Peter Pan. I had no idea how I would stay a kid, but tonight, this notion would safely carry me to sleep.

    From that prophetic night, the days journeyed on with no meaning until I found myself outside on a summer's day mowing the lawn. The sun shone brightly and the skies possessed not a single cloud among them. This was a day that made me savor the fact that I was a kid. My name was Ian Ramos and I was a thin but athletic African American who was now at the age of fifteen. My skin was a light brown texture that resembled caramel and I had a small afro on top of my head that usually remained uncombed. The topics that dominated my life were comics and baseball cards. I cherished the summer and loathed having to waste parts of it doing menial chores.

The summer air lingered with the scent of freshly cut grass, as I pushed our five-year-old mower through our lawn. As a cool, refreshing breeze blew by, I thought to myself, "Man, why does my dad always have to give me work when I have some days off? This is too good a day to waste having to mow the lawn." I shut off the mower and sat on the electrical box in our front yard. I rested on the box, taking notice of the kids playing in my neighborhood.

Across the street from my house, Mark, my five-year-old neighbor, threw an old, abused tennis ball against his garage and then caught it with his baseball glove, probably pretending he was in the seventh game of the World series. Some little girls in our neighborhood stood in the middle of our street bickering over some game they were playing. One thing our neighborhood had was an abundance of kids. Guajome, our street, had at least fifteen kids and our block probably had twenty, and yet having so many kids in the neighborhood I felt was a blessing, since I had grown up an only child.

I had lived in this neighborhood for almost two years, and I had lived in Southern California my whole life. I had witnessed the emergence and growth of a city, for what once had been my hometown by the name of Sunnymead had now quadrupled and been changed into the city Moreno Valley. Sunnymead was a town where people moved to get away from the urban areas. Moreno Valley was a city where you could stake a claim for a growing future. In fact, from what I heard,

Moreno Valley was the nation's fastest growing city at the time. I was two years old when my parents moved into our town. At that time, there were only two stores. Now there were hundreds. Everywhere there was open land; you could bet money on the fact that somewhere there were developers designing the architecture for the vacant property. We lived in a ranch filled with newly constructed suburban houses. The house we lived in now had just been built two years ago, and all the territory that surrounded our neighborhood was being leveled so that more tracts of houses could be built upon it. Personally, I liked the rural, untouched areas of Moreno Valley better.

While the kids played throughout my street, Guajome, my attention slid off the children and back to myself. I stood up on top of the electrical box and spread my arms out, imagining that I was a gigantic eagle flying over a vast canyon. Using my powerful wings, I gracefully soared though the heavens when I noticed an unsuspecting rabbit nibbling on a stem of grass. I flew through the skies, gliding on my wings, preparing myself for a heart-wrenching nosedive, but as I plummeted to the ground below, I remembered the chores that I had to do.

I jumped off the box and walked over to the lawn mower. I tugged on the mower's rope, trying to get its engine started. "Come on, you piece of junk," I said, as if my words themselves would start the machine.

As I tried to get the mower started, I heard some faint but familiar voices down the street. I looked down the street and saw two kids running around the corner; it was T.J. and Charles. They both ran over to my yard, breathing heavily, and once they were in my grass they struggled to catch their breath as if they had an important message to give me.

T.J., whose full name stood for Timothy James Sullivan, was one of my best friends. He lived on the street,

Catalejo, which ran into my street, Guajome. He was a white kid with dirty, blonde hair that reached down to his shoulders, and he could always be found wearing a T-shirt bearing his favorite heavy metal band and a pair of blue jeans that were ripped where his knees were. He was really the only person in the neighborhood around my age, since he was also fifteen and only three months younger than I was.

T.J. was probably the most untamed kid I had ever known. He was the symbol of youthful rebellion; he did what he wanted to do, when he wanted, and rarely thought about the consequences of his actions. He always had an uncanny knack for getting himself and others around him into trouble. Needless to say, parents, including mine, did not want their sons or daughters hanging around him.

Charles, on the other hand, was more of an acquaintance. He lived across the street from T.J.'s house. I did not hang around him too much. I just knew him as the kid with the pool table in his garage.

Once T.J. caught his breath, he looked over and said to me, "Ian, you have got to come with us."

"Why? What have you guys been doing?' I asked him.

"We were running from that security guard," T.J. said, not having fully regained his breath yet.

"He almost caught us too," Charles said.

I had seen the man they were referring to. He was a white male, who was probably in his mid-thirties, with rough skin that looked tougher than sandpaper and a thick, black mustache that matched the color of his hair. I was not fond of him, but then again, I also was not fond of most adults.

"What was he chasing you guys for? Did you guys do something?" I asked with curiosity.

"Nothin', we were just going to the school, when he got all pissed off at us," T.J. said. "You've gotta come back with us and check this guy out."

"I don't know," I said with a great deal of hesitance. I still had to finish my chores, and I did not want to get into any trouble with this security guard.

"Come on, Ian. Trust me," T.J. said, trying to reassure me.

My curiosity took control and I gave in, saying, "Well, o.k. Just let me go and put the mower away."

After I put the mower in the garage, the three of us walked down my street, Guajome, and over towards the construction site. "I hope he's not home," I thought to myself as we walked down the sidewalk. After a three-minute walk, we reached the construction area. About the size of a soccer field, the construction site was filled with lumber and other material that would some day house around twenty people. Towards the left end of the site stood the security guard's house. His house resembled an old gypsy wagon from some film made in the 50's. In reality it was an old school bus with a roof on top of it that had been transformed to look like a house, and the whole monstrosity from rooftop to wheels had been painted purple.

Underneath the trailer lay the man's pets: two white American Eskimo dogs. Both resembled large white wolves and both were now sound asleep underneath the man's house. Each was full grown and helped the security guard keep an eye on the neighborhood. My eyes then wandered away from the man's dogs to his vehicle. His automobile stood out almost as much as his house did. He owned an old, worn-down jeep, the kind that the military used for transportation. It had been painted a tarnished sort of yellow except for the doors and the hood, which were colored a creamy white. My mind suddenly jumped off the security guard's unique possessions and back to the situation at hand.

Now what do we do?" I asked, still half hoping he was not home.

"We've gotta make sure we're on that side of him, so we can get away if he comes out," T.J. said as he pointed to an area which lay centered between the construction site and the nearby Victoriano elementary school. The three of us walked over to the position T.J. had pointed to. My apprehension had vanished, and now my curiosity was running wild. I just hoped T.J. was not over-exaggerating, as he often would do.

"Now what do we do?" I asked T.J., hoping that this would not be disappointing.

"O.k., now, start screaming and making loud noises, as loud as you can," T.J. said.

"Are you sure?" I asked T.J.

"Trust me," was all he replied. He then moved his eyes away from mine and onto the man's trailer as he began yelling, "Hey, get your ugly butt out here and chase us!"

I moaned to myself in disbelief; this was T.J.'s idea of not angering the man. We all watched the trailer, not making a sound, waiting to see what would happen. The seconds went by without any movement from the trailer or sound from us until I asked, "Are you sure this guy was chasing you guys? Maybe he was running somewhere else or maybe he's not home."

I could tell T.J. did not even acknowledge my comments when he shouted, "Can't you hear me? I said get out here!" Then one of the dogs that had been sleeping began to stir, and when it saw us, it ran out from underneath the trailer and started barking at us, waking up the other dog. Having targeted us as the noisy interruption, both dogs crawled out from underneath the trailer and started running towards us at an alarming speed.

"Oh, crap, we're dead," I said in terror, but then the dogs were suddenly jerked back for some unknown reason. Then I noticed they were chained to the trailer.

Before I could let out a sigh of relief, the door from the trailer swung open. My eyes widened and my mouth dropped in shock. The security guard opened the door and came out wearing dark blue jeans and an old black t-shirt that looked like it had not been washed in months. The man stood at his doorway peering at us for what seemed a millennium. The security guard stood there staring, without one word advancing from his mouth, while the three of us stood there motionless. "What in the heck am I doing here?" I thought to myself, but before I could even attempt to answer my own thoughts, the man stepped down from the trailer, opened the door of his jeep, and sat in his vehicle.

T.J. finally broke our silence when he yelled, "Run for it!"

The three of us turned around and started sprinting away from the security guard. In the next instant, the jeep's engine roared to life like a lion that had just spotted its prey. I could see now what T.J.'s strategy was. If we made it to the fence that surrounded Victoriano Elementary School, the security guard would have to drive all the way around the block to get to the school, and by that time we could be at home eating lunch. I just hoped we made it to the fence in time.

As we sprinted towards the school, I thought to myself, "He's going to kill us. He's going to kill us." I turned my head and watched as dust flew up from the jeep's rear tires. "We are so dead," I said aloud. I then looked at T.J. and Charles and saw the terror in their faces. Their faces resembled the expressions of someone seated on a plane that was about to crash. As we ran, we ran over sheets of plywood, dodged beer bottles that had been left by construction workers and leaped over stacks of two by fours. Our only consolation was the fact that the man also had to steer around these obstacles. Unfortunately, the security guard maneuvered through the debris as if he had been doing it for years.

As I cleared a pile of wood, I spun my head quickly and saw that the man was gaining ground. I could tell that the others also could see this when Charles yelled out, "We're not going to make it!"

"Just keep running," I told him. The fence was right before us, but now the security guard was right behind us as. "Please let us make it. Please let us make it," I thought to myself. With the man right behind us I yelled out, "Jump for it!" We leaped onto the fence and then scurried up it like squirrels up a tree. Once at the top of the fence, we dove straight for the ground, impacting hard on the grass of the school yard. Two seconds later, I sat up, panting heavily, and asked, "You guys all right?"

T.J. and Charles were just picking their bodies off the grass when Charles responded, "Yah, we're o.k."

"See, I told you guys we'd make it," T.J. told us with a grin on his face.

The three of us then looked up towards the man. He was parked right in front of us on the opposite side of the fence. He shut off the engine, got out of his jeep, slammed the door and then motioned with his hands for us to come over to him.

"How dumb does this guy think we are?" I said to myself. After what we had just gone through to escape from him, there was no way that we were now going to waltz over to him and deliver ourselves to him.

"No way!' T.J. shouted as he stood up.

"Why don't you come over and get us, you Jeep Man?" I said, trying to antagonize him even further.

"Yah, why don't you come out and get us, Jeep Man?" Charles said as all three of us stood standing by the school yard. We stood in the soccer field that lay next to the basketball courts; by the courts stood the classroom buildings and on the other side of the courts was the neighborhood's most prized possession, the playground.

As my eyes moved from the playground over to the man, I watched as he stood by his jeep waiting for us to accept his moronic proposal. Seeing that the man was not even fidgeting, I whispered to T.J., "So how are we going to get back home with him just standing there?"

"We just sit here and wait for him to go back to his house," T.J. said, responding to my query.

We sat back on the grass for about two minutes waiting for the man to choose some course of action. I dug my fingers through the grass, as I became anxious to take some action of my own. Tired of waiting for the man, I asked, "So what do you think is with this guy? He's got a major problem."

"Aw, he just hates kids," T.J. said, giving his interpretation of the man. The man now walked inside his jeep and shut his door.

"Hey, look! He's getting back into his jeep. Do you think he's coming back to get us?" Charles asked.

"Well, even if he is, there's no way he can get us unless that jeep of his can fly over that fence," T.J. said, reassuring Charles. The man sat in his car, granting us no eye contact, restarted his engine and then drove off in the opposite direction.

"Good, he's gone. Now all we have to do is just wait to make sure he's not out there waiting for us," T.J. told us.

I was still confused on this whole matter. From what I had seen from this man today, he did not appear to be the kind of man who would surrender so easily. In fact, he had us exactly where he wanted us. In this position, we were at his disposal: prisoners awaiting their executioner.

Still as perplexed as ever, I asked, "What's he up to?"

"Don't worry about it, Ian. He's probably just going to the store or something," T.J. said, trying to calm my suspicions.

Maybe he was just going to Hughs, the local supermarket, for some food, or he could have just been leaving for some personal motive of his own, but I kept recalling how he gave us no eye contact. It was as if he had some secret scheme that he did not want us to figure out, and I knew from my avid comic book reading that evil villains would often feign defeat in order to get the upper hand against the unsuspecting hero. I stretched my eyes across the area, probing for some evidence that would support my presumption. I then began to survey the wall which surrounded our neighborhood. For the first few seconds, I found no indication of what I was searching for. I was about to abandon my idea, when I switched my eyes over to the left side of the main wall. For a brief moment, I unearthed what I thought I had been searching for. I saw what seemed to be the creamy white top of the man's jeep.

"O.k., you guys. Hurry up and climb over to the other side," I told them, hoping my accusations were correct.

"Are you crazy? What if he's still out there?" T.J. asked.

"He'll catch us for sure if we stay over here," I said, hoping that they would believe me.

"I don't know, Ian," T.J. said with a great deal of hesitancy in his voice.

"Well, you guys can stay here if you want to, but I'm going to the other side," I said, as I prayed that my accusations were accurate. I turned my back on them and began to climb the fence, and T.J. and Charles began climbing with me.

Once on the other side T.J. said, "You sure about this, Ian?"

"Pretty sure," I said, trying to hide my apprehension.

Then in the next moment, the man drove his jeep around one of the school buildings and into the school yard. Once he saw us, he parked on the school's basketball court, got out of the jeep, and stared at us in what I could tell was frustration. Seeing that our route home was now unguarded I said, "Come on. Let's go home." We departed from the construction site with no worries, for by the time the man returned we would be in T.J.'s living room playing Super Mario Brothers.

Later that night, after I left T.J.'s house, I lay in bed with my eyelids drooping over my eyes. I giggled softly to myself as I replayed the events that had taken place today. A feeling of confidence and bravado surged through my veins as I remembered the precise moment when I deduced this Jeep Man's plan to capture us. This Jeep Man could have sent us to prison, or maimed us or even have made us one with the road by running over us with that vehicle of his. The Jeep Man must have been hired to guard that territory, which must have meant that he was an experienced, proficient professional, yet we still managed to elude his grasp.

I felt as if I could take on an entire army of jeep men as I lay in the darkness. As I began to fall further asleep, for the first time I felt a glimmer of hope. Let death prepare herself for battle. I would defeat her the same way I had defeated this Jeep Man.

CHAPTER 2

The Feud

I awoke the next morning feeling rejuvenated, like a child after Christmas day - a child who thinks only of playing with his newly unwrapped toys. For the Jeep Man had dispensed presents of adventure and excitement for the good boys of our neighborhood. And now, visions of perilous quests and hazardous expeditions danced through my head as I lay in bed contemplating what I would do today.

I felt alive. I felt invulnerable. I wished there were an alligator nearby, so I could wrestle it to the ground and make it beg for submission. I wanted everyday to be a monumental adventure. That was how life should be. Life was not about wasting our precious time by staying up late working on some tedious geography report. It was not about making sure your room was kept presentable, and it was not about sitting in a monotonous classroom while life was outside flashing by us.

I stood up in my bed raising my right arm into the air pretending that I was on an archaic, pirate ship gripping a steel sword. On the other end of the ship stood the Jeep Man, wearing an eye patch and holding a blade of his own. The ship was adrift somewhere in the Pacific Ocean and a group of defiled, odorous pirates circled us waiting for the confrontation.

In the next instant, the Jeep Man charged me and with a loud bellow lunged his sword at my throat. The scum watching us cheered their approval as they screamed for blood. With lightning speed, I moved my steel in front of my throat, blocking his attack and hindering the introduction of his metal to my flesh. Our swords entangled, and I moved my left foot up to his chest and kicked him back a few feet. "Is that the best you can do?" I asked in an egotistical tone. Engulfed with rage, he charged once again, this time thrusting his sword deep into my abdomen. "He got me," I muttered in agony. The pirates stood silent, as I fell back on my bed and into reality as the ship disappeared.

I could not just keep a courageous spirit like mine bottled up. Like a titillating secret, it had to be shared. I wanted to bestow it upon my closest companion. I got out of bed, put my contact lenses in, and threw on a pair of shorts and an old, worn out T-shirt. I went downstairs, where I prepared breakfast for myself. I quickly gobbled down two scrambled eggs and engulfed a glass of cranberry juice.

After finishing the last morsel of my breakfast I headed out the door. I had a few hours of freedom, since my parents would not be back home from their work till six o'clock. Closing the door behind me, I strolled across the street and knocked on the door of my friend Dan.

Daniel Green was my best friend on the planet, which was kind of abnormal since I was four years older than he was. Dan was an eleven-year-old kid who had moved from Oregon to California. He was extremely pale, and he consisted of practically nothing but skin and bones. He had dark brown hair which looked almost black and was styled in the 1950's church boy look.

As I stood by his front door, I looked through the window and saw him lying on the carpet eating a bowl of cereal while watching television. Once he heard the knock, he left his bowl and walked up to the door, unlocked it and opened the door. "Hey, Ian," he said as I walked into his house and sat on his couch. "What have you been up to?"

"Nothing much. But I've been dying to tell you what we did yesterday," I said eagerly.

"What did you do?" Dan asked as he lay back down on the floor and began finishing his bowl of cereal.

"And I can't wait for you to meet the Jeep Man," I told him.

"The who?" Dan asked, checking to see if I pronounced the name right.

I explained to him, "The Jeep Man. You know; it's that security guard guy who lives by the school, where they make houses. He was chasing us yesterday, and boy, was it fun."

"He was chasing you? What did you guys do? Who was with you?" he asked as he slurped the remaining milk out of his bowl.

"Well, it was me, T.J. and Charles. We were over by the houses and I guess we're not supposed to be over there or something. So he got all mad and chased us. You have got to come with me. It's more fun than anything," I said as I watched a doubting expression grow on Dan's face.

Dan had a tendency to worry too much about certain situations that involved a risk or chance. He was always afraid that he might get himself into trouble or some other form of mischief, which was kind of odd, since his parents were the most lenient parents in the neighborhood. Then whenever a risky situation reared its head, you could always count on Dan to give every excuse, reason and justification on why he should not participate in that certain situation.

"I don't know, Ian. We could get in tons of trouble," Dan said.

"We won't get in trouble, because we won't get caught," I told him.

"If my parents found out, they would get real mad at me," Dan said, continuing with the excuses.

"Don't worry. No one's going to be telling your parents," I said, trying to reassure him.

"I don't know. I could get in lots of trouble," Dan said.

"Just come on. You'll have the most fun in your whole life," I said, as I continued to wear out his excuses.

"Well..." he said with a long pause.

"Come on," I said, trying to help motivate him.

Then, after finishing his long pause, an "Okay" slowly came out of his mouth.

"Good, let's go," I said ready to leave that instant.

Dan placed his bowl in the kitchen sink, grabbed his high tops, opened the door and yelled, "I'm gonna be with Ian, Mom." He shut the door and began lacing his shoes, asking, "So, where are we going now?"

"Well, first we've got to go and get T.J. Then we'll go head over to the Jeep Man's house," I said to him as we walked up Guajome. We were almost up to Catalejo, T.J.'s street, when we heard the sound of rubber wheels rolling against the pavement. T.J. then glided around the corner on top of his skateboard with Charles walking alongside him.

"Hey, where you guys going?" T.J. asked as he rolled up to us.

"We were just getting ready to see you," I told him.

"And we were gonna see you," Charles told me.

"Yah, I wanted to show the Jeep Man to Dan," I said eagerly.

"Cool, let's go," T.J. said. "We wanted to go see the Jeep Man anyway."

"You know, we could just go play basketball or do some video games," Dan said, trying to pull everyone's attention away from the Jeep Man.

"Don't tell me you're chicken," T.J. said, seeing through Dan's ruse.

"I just don't want to get in any trouble," Dan said, trying to justify his feelings.

T.J.'s temper surfaced as he scolded, "Man, don't be such a wussy. We're not going to get in any trouble."

I could sense an immense tongue-lashing brewing, so for Dan's sake I interrupted and said, "Let's hurry up and go, before the guy leaves or something."

T.J. dropped his skateboard in Dan's yard next to his welcome mat. Then, the four of us turned around and started walking down Guajome. We walked down the street until we came upon the construction area. We then proceeded to make our way to the Jeep Man's house. A few feet away from the man's house, we crouched down and hid behind a stack of plywood.

"Well, there's his jeep," Charles said pointing out the obvious.

"So now we know he's home or at least somewhere in the neighborhood," I said, trying to figure out exactly where the Jeep Man might be.

"You ready, Ian?" T.J. asked.

"Yah, let's go for it," I said as I glanced over at Dan. He was fidgeting nervously as he took in a deep breath. He looked like someone who was about to be forced to go on his first roller coaster ride. I started to feel a little guilty, but then I just thought of the rush he would feel after our exciting escapade was over.

T.J. and I stood up and walked around the stack of wood as Charles and Dan followed closely behind us. Once ready, T.J. began yelling, "Hey, we're back, you stupid ugly jeep guy. Why don't you see if you can get us this time?" T.J. said in a sarcastic tone.

Unlike the day before, this time the Jeep Man appeared immediately. He opened the door and stood there glaring at the four of us. Two seconds ago, I felt as brave and invincible as one of my favorite superheroes, but now I stood scared and intimidated, wishing I had stayed inside the warmth of my covers this morning. There was something uncanny about being in the presence of the Jeep Man. Power filled with an aura of mystery seemed to surround him. Standing before him, I was frozen once again. I could not even swallow the saliva that was building rapidly inside my mouth.

I snapped back to a conscious state when Charles whispered, "What's he doing?"

"Whatever it is, we're about to find out," I said, hoping the Jeep Man would go back inside his trailer.

"I don't care what he does. I'm not scared of him," T.J. said, trying to sound confident.

"You think there's still time to go back?" Dan asked. It was too late though, for I knew that there could be only two outcomes for this scenario. We would either elude the Jeep Man or be captured by him. There would be no withdrawal.

I disregarded Dan's remarks as I watched the Jeep Man. He was holding some pieces of rope that went underneath his house. He gave the ropes a light tug, and his ultimate weapons surfaced. His two colossal white canines appeared outside the trailer. Standing at the Jeep Man's side they awaited their master's command to rip us into shreds. The Jeep Man had been pushed too far. He wasn't playing now.

"Oh, crap! He's gonna sic his dogs on us," Charles yelled.

"The fence! Go for the fence!" I screamed, wishing I could magically teleport to the other side of the fence.

The four of us turned around and dashed toward the fence. As I ran towards our salvation, I could hear the patter of paws slapping against the earth. I could feel the breath of my predators on my legs. All thoughts vanished from my head; only my survival instincts remained.

Dan, as terrified as I was, looked at me and said, "Ian, I want to go home!"

"Just go the fence!" I managed to blurt out.

"They're gonna get me!" Dan yelled as the four of us leaped onto the fence. We quickly scrambled up. While T.J. and Charles had safely jumped to the other side of the fence, Dan had accidentally bumped into me at the top of the fence and sent us plummeting to the ground below. I landed on the side of my hip while Dan landed a few inches away from me. Luckily, we had landed on the safe side of the fence.

Not having time to acknowledge the pain, I spun my head around expecting to see the beasts gnashing at the fence hoping to get a piece of us. Instead I saw the Jeep Man about twenty feet away still holding the dogs by their leashes. My worries did not fade though, for now he was marching this way. We all stared helplessly, as our nemesis walked towards us. But then, a peculiar twist of fate happened. He stopped. He started pacing back and forth. Something obviously was floating in the Jeep Man's head.

Dan tapped on my left shoulder and said, "I want to go home."

"How do you think you're gonna get home with him watching us like that?" T.J. asked. I scanned the area, searching for some escape route. Wherever we went, the Jeep Man would surely follow. The only safe path that I saw was to go around the fence and then climb over the wall that encircled our neighborhood. Of course, the Jeep Man would not let us go this easily.

Yet he might just let some of us leave, and then I would be able to safely escort Dan home. Evading the Jeep Man was going to be complicated and this would be too perilous a journey for Dan. Plus if anything happened to us, Dan would have to be our last line of defense. This did not too sound reassuring to me, but my options, like our escape routes, were scarce.

"Well, I'm going to take Dan home real quick. Then I'll come back and help you guys," I told them.

"O.k., I'll see you when you get back" T.J. said, giving Dan a disgruntled glare.

"Charles and T.J. behind. Luckily, as I had prayed, the Jeep Man held his ground, keeping a close eye on T.J. It seemed that the Jeep Man had some hidden grudge towards T.J.

Hopefully, we would never uncover the reason. We walked past the basketball courts, the playground, and the softball field until we came upon the massive white wall that surrounded our entire ranch. At four feet tall, we quickly climbed the wall and then began to walk home. "At least this seems to be working," I thought to myself. I just hoped T.J. and Charles had the sense to stay put until I returned.

Finally, the wall opened up and let us into our block. We headed down the street making our way to Catalejo as the hum of an engine began to draw closer.

"Do you think that's...?" Dan asked me.

"The Jeep Man. It could be," I told him, hoping I was wrong.

As the hum grew louder, my heart rate began to quicken while my muscles tensed. We were out in the open. There wasn't an object large enough to keep the Jeep Man at bay. If this was the Jeep Man, he could snatch us up before Dan could let out a scream.

"He's coming, Ian!" Dan yelled.

Options scrambling through my head. I yelled, "Behind those bushes!"

The two of us dived behind one of our neighbor's bushes. My elbows hit the ground with an alarming force, but I ignored the pain and peered through the bush to see just who our pursuer was. It was definitely a jeep. It was a brand new black jeep that had probably just been taken off the assembly line. I rubbed my elbow, knocking off the tiny rocks that had lodged themselves in my skin. "Come on," I said. "Let's hurry up and go home."

We made our way down Catalejo, and then onto Guajome and then over to Dan's house. "Did you wanna come in?" Dan asked.

"No, I'd better go back and see how T.J.'s doing," I told him. "And if we're not back in twenty minutes, you'll have to come and get us."

"Me?" Dan asked doubtfully.

"Yah," I said as I started to leave his house. If luck was on our side, T.J. might have already thwarted the man's schemes and would be on his way back now. I waved good-bye to Dan and jogged back towards the construction area. Once I reached the corner, I gasped in shock. T.J. and Charles stood beside the ghastly trailer with the Jeep Man hovering over them. The Jeep Man had caught T.J. and Charles and was now conversing with them. Part of me wanted to tuck my tail in between my legs, run home and hide beneath my bedcovers, but I could not leave T.J. at the mercy of the Jeep Man.

I had to think quickly. Perhaps a diversion would give the others a chance to escape. I poked my head out, trying to get a better view of the situation. At that moment, T.J. spotted me. The time for thinking was over; action was now called for. But before I could make a move, T.J. yelled out, "Ian, come on over."

"What is T.J. doing?" I thought to myself. The Jeep Man turned his head toward me. T.J. had given up my position. My mind told me to run, but the message was not making it to my legs.

"Don't worry. It's all right," T.J. said.

T.J.'s statement did not reassure me. Maybe in the short time I was gone, the Jeep Man had brainwashed T.J., turning T.J.'s will into his own. This was the only explanation I could think of for T.J.'s apparent betrayal. But for some ludicrous reason, I had faith in T.J. I stepped out of the corner and began walking towards the Jeep Man. My brain pleaded with my legs to turn around, but my legs kept moving forward. I gritted my teeth and tried to keep my legs from wobbling. Now I stood before the Jeep Man, my face aimed straight at the ground, for I dared not look the Jeep Man in the eye.

In a sturdy tone the Jeep Man said, "Now, as I was telling these two, I'll consider this time a warning. It is my job to make sure no one goes in this area. A kid got killed before by falling debris from houses just like these. I know you guys don't want to go around this area when you go to the school, but that's what you're going to have to do."

With the lecture over, the three of us nodded our heads approvingly, turned around and headed home. I looked over at T.J. and he had a devilish grin on his face. I did not have to ask him what he was thinking; his expression said it all. This would not be our last meeting with the Jeep Man. He would not get the best of us so easily. The Jeep Man's words had fallen on deaf ears.

Ignoring the Jeep Man's pleas, we had become wanted men - outlaws any time we set foot upon the construction site. As the weeks passed, the Jeep Man chased us all over the neighborhood. Only by crafty and ingenious plans did we manage to escape. Of course, the Jeep Man had his moments. There were times when the Jeep Man was so close to catching us I swear I could feel his breath on the back of our necks, but usually some sort of luck bailed us out at the last minute. One thing was certain though, catching us was now on the list of the Jeep Man's top priorities, and I would not have wanted it any other way.

CHAPTER 3

A Second Home

I wore a coat of perspiration as my heart pounded, trying to bulldoze its way through my chest while my veins lay exposed for all eyes to see. I had been trained for this for over half a decade. Running, or cross-country, had become second nature, but I loathed it with an intense passion. It ranked right up there with broccoli and algebra homework. I felt like nothing more than a purebred. I despised everything - the hours of training, the vomit-producing sport drinks, the six morning workouts, the unbearable pain of pushing my lungs past their limit and the stress it put upon me. Cross-country was the only sport known to man that was completely devoid of any form of fun, but I brushed aside my feelings as Dan and I ran through the neighborhood.

"Ignore the pain. That's the key to being a good runner," I told Dan and my tiring legs.

"How many miles do you think we've run?" Dan asked.

"'Bout two and a half," I told him as I silently marveled at Dan's ability to keep up.

"I think I'm finally getting used to this running. It's not so tough," Dan said, struggling to talk and breathe simultaneously.

Of course I had to maintain my image. I could not let Dan think my torturous sport was so easy. I looked around the neighborhood, searching for a suitable challenge for Dan, and then I saw it. "You haven't seen anything yet. Let's go to the hill for a real workout," I told him.

The hill I was referring to lay next to a set of mountains which separated Moreno Valley from Lake Perris. While the hill was gigantic, the mountains were colossal. It seemed as if they reached up to the heavens and kissed the clouds. Both the mountain and the hill had their skins coated with cactuses, bushes and tumbleweeds, and had boulders and rocks which were embedded in the mountain, like chocolate chips in a cookie.

The hill had visited me many times in my nightmares. To get extra practice at cross- country running, I had spent hours there sprinting up the hill till my legs felt like committing suicide. This torture chamber would surely be too much for Dan.

As we jogged our way over to the hill a familiar distant voice cried out, "Hey, you guys, wait up!" We turned our heads and saw T.J. and his younger brother Cory roller-blading toward us.

Although Corey Sullivan physically resembled a ten-year-old version of T.J. with nicely trimmed hair, mentally Corey was nothing like his older brother. At ten years old, he had an imagination that would make novelists jealous. Sometimes he'd stay inside all day building weird contraptions with items from his house. He was probably the only person I viewed as more creative than myself.

Once they caught up to us, Dan and I stopped to catch our breath. "Where you guys goin?" I asked.

T.J. looked at Dan and said, "Your sister told us you were out here, so we thought we'd come with you guys."

"So where are you guys going?" Corey asked.

"We're going to that hill over there," Dan told them. "Do you guys want to come?'

"Sure, let's go," T.J. said.

I was glad T.J. was going with us. He always seemed to sprinkle a little bit of spice on the situation at hand. In fact, I had never taken any of my friends to this hill before. I had always traveled alone or with my father.

We crossed the street and walked past the old dried-up canal. Whenever we had extreme amounts of rain, the canal helped take the city's excess water into the ranch's man-made lake that lay across the street. During summer, though, it remained useless and served the dual purpose of scenery and shelter for rodents.

From the canal, we crossed the street and came upon the valley of dirt that lay at the base of the mountain. It stretched out over a mile before finally reaching the foot of the hill. After walking a few minutes, we came across a canyon that deterred us from the hill. Because it was around six feet deep, we decided to walk around it until we found a more suitable height at which we could cross. Taking this detour, we walked along the man-made lake until the canyon had dissipated. From there, it took us about fifteen minutes before we reached the path that would take us to the peak of the hill.

Not wanting to rest until we were finished, the four of us quickly started up the pathway. About halfway there, a sweaty Dan commented, "Man, this is hard."

"Yah, and we're just walking up it. You should try running up this," I told him.

"You two should try it like this," T.J. said. T.J. and Corey were carrying their roller blades while walking up the hill on just the soles of the roller blades.

"I thought it'd be pretty hard for you guys to get up there in those," I told them.

"Well, at least we're at the top now," Dan said. We were not actually at the top. The path went further up in another direction but our current position lay flat like a valley and was one of the few spots that were void of any tumbleweeds, bushes or cactuses. Next to this empty lot stood three boulders.

The first boulder was as tall as a house and yielded an abundant amount of shade. The second boulder was actually half a boulder. Somehow, it had been split in half and was now half the size of the first boulder; it lay about three feet in front of the first one. The third boulder stood adjacent to the first one except it was two or three inches taller.

"Come on, you guys. Let's go sit over here," Corey said eagerly, wanting to rest his feet from the soles of the roller blades. We climbed upon the split boulder and sat down. This was the perfect resting area, for the shade from the huge boulder covered the entire area. The shade also seemed to ease our bodies from the long walk up the hill.

As my body recuperated I looked out over the boulder and said, "Wow, look at that!" You could see all of Moreno Valley. I could see our ranch's lake, the military base, the airport and even the planes in them. This was a perfect lookout.

"And look at those!" Corey said.

We turned our heads and gazed at the mountains Corey was referring to. They were magnificent. They stood gallantly demanding respect. In all my comings, I had never noticed the splendor of the hill and the mountains. They were astounding and actually laid our tongues to rest for a few seconds.

As I stood there admiring God's creation, a memory leaped into my head. "Hey, Yonik's older brother Paul once said that a plane crashed up there before, and he went up there and saw it!" I told them enthusiastically.

"Cool," T.J. said.

"Neat," followed Dan.

Next an idea appeared in my head. It was the kind of idea that makes men into Nobel Prize winners. "Tomorrow, let's climb it and go look at that crashed plane," I told them.

I could see the enthusiasm in me mirrored in them as T.J. said, "Yah, we can bring a whole bunch of stuff up there."

"We'll bring food and water too." Corey said.

"This is going to be so cool!" I said.

"Tomorrow's gonna be bitchin'," T.J. said eagerly.

We headed back down the path as visions of excitement danced through my head. I could see the four of us searching through the wreckage now. I was inspecting the cockpit and had found two rotting skeletons sitting in the charred seats. These bones must have belonged to the pilot and co-pilot, for both lay hunched over the controls. Dan yelled for me to come to the back of the plane. I ran towards him curious to see what the commotion was about. I then saw that the hull of the plane was filled to the brim with wooden crates that read 'Top Secret.' I pulled out a screwdriver from the backpack I had brought with me. I jammed it in the crate and began to pry it open. Just before the top came off and I could see what was inside one of the crates, my dream burst as Dan said to me, "Man, tomorrow is going to be so much fun."

"I know. I can't wait," I told him as we finally hit the sidewalk and began making our way back home.

Next morning, after a prolonged night due to my eagerness, we gathered together in my driveway, counting and checking our supplies. In the driveway lay my large green tent, five water bottles, my lucky red backpack, two duffel bags, two sacks of food and one piece of wood. I was very fortunate that my parents worked on weekdays. With my mother working for the county of Riverside and my father working for a computer company in Anaheim, most of my summer days were unregulated. If my parents had spent more time at home, days like this could never have occurred, for my father would never let me go to the hill during the summertime. He always said there were too many snakes up there during the daytime. But I would not let a little thing like feeble rattlesnakes hinder me from seeing the wreckage of that plane.

"Hey, you guys all ready?" our friend James asked.

"We're just making sure we've got everything," Dan told him. James Farabelli was about a year older than Dan and one of the first people I had met over here. He was around the same height as Dan, with short, black, curly hair. James leaned toward the chubby side but made up for it with his athletic ability.

    James and his family had moved out here all the way from Pennsylvania for a new job. Back in Pennsylvania his father was a reverend, so James was somewhat of a choirboy. But the influence of T.J. and California were definitely having an effect on him. I was not sure if he was going to make it today. His father was extremely strict, and sending your kid off with T.J. for the day was not on a parent's wish list.

    "Okay, we got everything," Corey said.

    "This is going to be so much fun!" I said. "You guys ready?"

    "Yah," James said.

    "Good, let's go," T.J. said. I put on my lucky backpack and then the five of us packed up the remaining equipment and headed toward the hill. On the way, we talked of the fun and excitement we would have on our hiking trip, trying to forget the heavy load each of us were carrying. Before we knew it, twenty minutes had disappeared as we walked down the street and around the construction area. From there, we walked through the field that lay adjacent to the school. Then we passed the dried-up canal, walked around the gorge, hiked up the main path and were now at the top of the hill. We began laying down the equipment, releasing heavy sighs.

    Dan threw his sports bag down and said, "Man, my back was killing me."

    "Yah, mine too," Corey told him.

    "At least we're finally up here," I told him.

    "Hey, it is nice up here," James said, having seen the hill and the mountains for the first time.

    "Let's hurry up and set this stuff up," T.J. said.

    "I know; then we can go and climb that baby," I said energetically.

We took the tent out of its bag and laid it out on an area where there were no bushes or cactuses. We then took out the poles and the stakes and began erecting the tent. And after ten minutes had passed, my large green tent stood tall, a testament to great campers everywhere. After we finished admiring the tent, we walked over to the split boulder, sat down, took out our sack lunches and began eating.

"I can't wait to climb up that mountain," T.J. said.

"How long do you think it'll take us?" Dan asked the group.

"Probably a long time," I said, answering his question. "Pass me that piece of wood, James."

James picked up the piece of wood that we had brought with us and said, "What did you bring that for, anyway?"

"I thought it'd be cool if we all carved our names and the date into it. Then we'll hide it up here and years from now we'll come back and get it," I told him, laying out my master plan.

"That's a perty good idea," James said.

"T.J., let me see your Dad's knife," I told him.

"Here," T.J. said as he pulled out a Swiss Army knife. I pulled the knife out and began carving an "I".

"It's not so tough," I thought to myself. "Too bad I was planning on becoming a superhero when I got older, otherwise I might have a real career in this carving thing." Once I finished inscribing the three letters of my name, I blew off the sawdust and examined my creation.

"Marvelous," I thought to myself. "A masterpiece in under ten minutes."

I then handed the wood over to Corey, who carved three letters before needing T.J. to help him finish the remaining two. Next, James carved his whole name in it before passing it over to T.J., who, once finished, handed it over to Dan. Once the names were completed, I then engraved the date underneath our names. Once finished, the wood read "Ian Corey Dan T.J. James July 7, 1991."

"Now we gotta find a good place to put it. Somewhere where no one can ever mess with it," I told the guys. We all inspected the area looking for the proper place.

I could hide it under the split boulder but that would be too accessible. I began to look down the hill for a more suitable hiding spot when Corey said, "I know where we can put it." All eyes turned toward him. "See those rocks?" he said pointing to some rocks between the first and the third boulder. "We can use those as steps, climb up and hide it up there. Come on. I'll show you." He grabbed the piece of wood and began walking up the boulder using the rocks for steps as he had said. T.J. quickly followed, and then the two disappeared for about ten seconds. While they were up top the rest of us quickly began brushing the dirt out of the tent. Corey then yelled out, "Hey, there's tons of cracks up here where we can hide it."

Once James, Dan and I finally finished cleaning the interior of the tent, T.J. came down, followed by his brother, and said, "We hid it somewhere good where no one will ever find it."

"Good work," I said to Corey. His ingenuity had come through again. This boy was destined to be an ingenious inventor. "Now that we took care of that, we should start heading up the mountain." We put the remaining water left inside the water bottles into the backpack, put the backpacks on, and began to make our way down the hill to get to the mountain. After a ten- minute trot down the hill, we reached the bottom of the mountain. The five of us looked up and began noticing the height to the top of the mountain.

"This is gonna be a long trip," Dan said as he eyed the mountain.

"I know, and don't forget to not look up," I told the four of them. Today at noon there was supposed to be a partial eclipse of the sun. I had heard horror stories of kids who had tragically gone blind from looking directly into the sun during an eclipse. It was almost noon and the grayish sky looked as if the eclipse was beginning to occur.

"Well, let's go," I said as the four of us set our feet upon the mountain.

"There aren't any paths," said Dan, as observant as ever.

"We make our own paths," I told him as I walked through a patch of tumbleweeds. "It's more fun without paths anyway." Covered from head to toe with prickly bushes and large tumbleweeds, the mountain was more treacherous than the hill. This also made it seem more adventurous. The great explorers Lewis and Clark did not follow any paths when they explored early America. Marco Polo never used trails when he explored the globe. The tougher the hardship, the bigger was the adventure. Perhaps on the mountain I would discover some long-lost colony. I could be the Christopher Columbus of Moreno Valley.

My grand delusions were interrupted when I saw T.J., James and Dan staring up into the sky. "You guys wanna go blind or somethin'?" I reminded them as I put my hands on top of a small boulder, preparing to climb it. "Don't you guys know what could...Hey, cut that out!" I said, warning James of the imminent danger. "You guys will be...Stop that!" I told Dan. But I realized it was hopeless; in the future I was bound to be the friend of four blind men.

Leaving the dire fates of my friends behind, we continued up the mountain with continuous cries of, "Did you see that rabbit?" and "Look at that hawk!" And every ten minutes or so Dan would swear he heard a rattlesnake nearby. But we proceeded, and as I pleaded with my comrades to keep their eyes away from the sky, we plowed through tumbleweeds filled with razor-like bristles that left marks on our legs. We climbed over rocks that stood two times our height. We crawled under branches and jumped over cactuses. We were all pretty worn out when Dan said, "My legs are killing me."

"Mine too," Corey said.

Our ankles were on fire, and the pain was not due to exhaustion. The cactus and tumbleweeds had left their marks upon us. Each step was a reminder of the mountain's brutality. "Let's sit down over here for a while," I said, referring to a large nearby rock. We sat upon the rock and took our shoes off and saw that our socks were drenched with sharp thorns and spiky thistles. Only T.J. did not have as many as the rest of us, since he was fortunate enough to have worn pants while the rest of us had worn shorts. We began plucking the pokers from our socks, hoping to relieve our feet from some of the pain. Five minutes had passed, and it seemed that our socks had as many pokers as they originally had had. The task was impossible. It was like trying to count the stars; there were just too many.

After taking a few sips from our water bottle, we put our shoes back on and started back on our hike. We leaped from boulder to boulder; we walked through grassy valleys where the stems of the grass reached our thighs. And after each hill we climbed, another one would emerge behind it, beckoning us to it. Two hours had passed, when we found ourselves in front of a hill which seemed to be fashioned of stone. In reality, it was an immensely vast boulder embedded into the mountain. It was as tall as a two-story house and as wide as a basketball court.

"That's kind of steep," Corey said, commenting on the rock's attributes.

"I know," Dan agreed. "Maybe we should go around it?"

"Damn, you are the biggest wussie," T.J. told Dan.

"It'll take too long to go around it. It'll be more fun climbin' it," I told him.

"Come on, let's go," T.J. said impatiently.

"Wait, I brought some rope and we can use it like real rock climbers do," I said as I passed out the strands of rope to them. "This way, if one of us falls, the four of us will stop him." Each of us tied the rope around our waists and gave the end to someone else who in turn tied the rope around his waist. We then got on our knees and began crawling up the colossal stone. For some unknown reason, my mind kept playing a scene from a movie I had recently watched. A man was on top of a building running from the police, and seeing he was cornered, he pulled out his revolver in order to retaliate. One of the cops was quicker though, and pulled out his gun and winged the fugitive in the left arm. The fugitive lost his balance and fell over the building, plummeting story after story until he slammed into the pavement.

I cleared my throat and prayed, "Just let us make it to the top. Just let us make it to the top." But just then, as if my prayer had gone unanswered, I saw Corey slip. Tiny bits of gravel flew from underneath his foot. Not sure if Corey would lose his grip or not, T.J. reached out and grabbed Corey's shirt before he lost his balance.

"Be careful," T.J. told his brother.

I began wondering what would have happened if Corey had slipped harder. And as I let my mind wander, my hand lost hold of the water bottle I had been carrying. Dan grabbed my arm, reassuring us that I would not take the same trip as my bottle. We watched as my bottle ricocheted down the stone, landing with a tremendous impact, the lid opening up and water spilling out.

I took a long breath and whispered, "Wow." Getting a good grasp, Dan and I resumed the climb. Then, in about two minutes, we pulled ourselves to the top of the stone. We untied the rope, pulled off our backpacks and laid them on the ground.

"Finally," Dan said in exhaustion.

"Man, look how high we are," James said.

"Wow! Look how far we've come," I responded. We gazed down over the stone and noticed the altitude and the distance we had traveled. "We've gotta get a picture of this." T.J. scavenged through my backpack and pulled out James' camera. James, Dan and I stood side be side with our arms over each other, posing for the picture, when Dan asked, "Hey, where's Cory?" In our current state of euphoria, we had forgotten all about him.

We looked and saw Cory lying on the ground all huddled up, crying. "What's wrong, Core?" T.J. asked, showing true concern.

Cory responded, "It's too high! It's too high!"

"We're almost there," T.J. said, trying to console him.

"It's too high!" was Cory's only response.

"What do we do now?" James asked.

"Maybe we should go back," Dan said. "I mean, we are pretty high."

"But we came all this way," I said. This was too intense of an adventure to just turn around and walk away from it.

"I'll stay with Cory," T.J. said as Cory stood up and wiped the tears from his cheek.

"And I'll stay with T.J.," Dan said, showing the cowardly, craven attitude we had grown so accustomed to.

"Well, I'm going up to the top," I said. "You guys just wait here."

"I'm coming with you," James said.

"O.k., we'll see you guys on the way back," I said as we took off, not looking back. James and I headed up the mountain and started the hike once again.

Now the hike was either beginning to get a little bit easier or I was becoming accustomed to the intense pain. James and I trudged on; the only thing that mattered was completing the adventure. We repeatedly climbed hills, only to find another hill waiting for us. An hour had passed, when we reached the top of a hill and saw a peculiar sight. There was not another hill to climb! We had hit the peak of the mountain. With screams of "We made it!" coming from our lips, we jumped and danced around proclaiming our victory.

I had seen no sight of the plane wreckage, but did not care as I looked down at the tiny city and yelled, "Look at me, world!"

I could see the ant-like figures of T.J., Dan and Corey buzzing around making noise. They obviously could see that we had reached the summit. I looked over at James and said, "We've gotta get some pictures of this." James pulled out the camera and each of us took turns taking pictures of us at the astounding altitude.

After the adrenaline rush had faded somewhat, I said, "Now comes the easy part - going back down." Then we finished up the remaining water bottle and headed back down. We could see T.J., Dan, and Cory making their way to the bottom. "Let's go over here. If we go this way we can beat 'em on the way down," I said, referring to what my eyes had picked up on as a short-cut.

As we continued down the alternate path, I heard a loud rustle in a bush a couple of yards away. I turned my head and my mouth dropped in amazement. For a couple of seconds, a full-grown deer stood staring at me. Then, in the next instant it turned and sprinted away around some large boulder.

It was the most awe-inspiring, spectacular sight I had ever witnessed. It had happened so fast, yet at the same time it seemed like an eternity. I had never seen a wild animal that was truly free. The ones I had witnessed were either on television or behind some confining cage. This deer was truly beautiful. "D..Did you see that?" I managed to spout out.

"I saw its back," James said.

"Hurry, before it's gone!" I said, running off toward the area where the deer had stood. I had to see it again. We sprinted to the area, but nothing was to be found. We searched with our eyes in all directions, but nothing could be found. "Oh well, boy, was that neat!"

"I know. I can't wait to tell the others," James said.

We got back on our shortcut and headed back down. We were now traveling at an alarming speed. "Going down is sure way easier than going up," I told James. About forty-five minutes passed before we hit the bottom.

"Hey, look over there," James said, pointing to T.J., Dan and Corey. They were just coming off the mountain. We all ran up to each other and T.J. said, "So how was it?"

James and I looked over at each other as I blurted out, "It was the coolest thing ever, you guys. We saw a deer up there, a real one!" Their mouths dropped.

"It was so cool," James said. We finished the story on the way back to the hill. Once we got there we packed up our equipment, took down the tent and headed down the hill. Luckily, Dan's mom, who had been worried about the five of us, had parked out in the street waiting for our arrival; we hopped in their truck and headed home.

It had been an amazing day. The mountain held millions of possibilities. There was so much exploring and adventuring to be done on the mountain. This would be only our first day. This was a kid's paradise. The hill and the mountain quickly became a "hang out" for all of us. We'd spend our summer months exploring the mountain and hanging out at the hill. The mountain became one of our main bases of operations, but to me it was more like a second home.

It was a home where I could set aside my worries and leave the confines of my drab society behind. Most importantly, it was the one place where I could contemplate death and would not be afraid. I would spend hours reflecting on the meaning of life and my role in it.

For going to the mountain was like taking a portal to another world. Fear had no authority and death was out of its jurisdiction. For this land was mine. Here, I was emperor. Here, I was master. Here, I would unearth death's secrets.

CHAPTER 4

The Dragon Lady

The hum of air conditioners buzzed through our neighborhood while the melodies of ice cream trucks flowed through the streets. The temperature rose well above one hundred degrees, as Moreno Valley passed through an intolerable heat wave. It was as if the sun had moved within a few yards from the earth.

On this blistering day, T.J., Dan and I walked toward our community pool in the ranch hoping to forget about the summer heat for a while. We walked down Guajome, then sneaked through the Jeep Man's construction area. We strolled through Victoriano School, crossed the street and then found ourselves outside of the ranch's recreation center. Our ranch's recreation center had basketball courts, a man-made lake, a steamy Jacuzzi and a large pool, yet we were there for only one reason.

"Finally, we're here. I'm dying," Dan said sarcastically.

"I know. I can't wait to get in that pool," I said, wiping a layer of sweat from my forehead.

"When we go, let's see if we can get those diving toys," T.J. said, referring to the diving toys that the people in the main office handed out.

For once, toys were not in the forefront of my mind. Thoughts of cool, brisk water dousing my blistering body plagued me. "Come on, guys. Let's take the quick way," I said, wanting to climb over the gate instead of walking around it. Enclosing the entire recreation center were metallic bars meant to keep anyone not living in the ranch from using the ranch's facilities.

"Maybe we should just walk around like we're supposed to. That way we won't get in any trouble," Dan said.

"Heck, no. I'm tired of walking," I told him. "And we won't get in any trouble. Right T.J.?" I said, asking for his assurance.

"Let's just walk around, 'cause I don't want 'em sending me home after we walked all the way here," T.J. said. The summer heat must have really been affecting T.J.'s brain. Usually, T.J. would be eager to commit any sinful act, and then he'd cuss Dan out for not wanting to participate. This was a boy whose sole purpose in life was to break all the rules any way he could. Perhaps aliens had kidnapped T.J. overnight and left a dull clone of him in his place.

After giving T.J. a questioning glance, I said, "Hey, if you guys want to walk all the way around, you can. I'll be inside doing cannonballs in the pool." I pulled myself to the top of the bars, hurled myself over and landed with the grace of an alley cat. I quickly looked around to see if anyone had noticed me.

I was a submarine commander on a top-secret mission, and I had just stolen vital information from the enemy. Having escaped from the enemy's penitentiary, leaving some of my fellow soldiers behind, I skulked through the docks searching for a boat to take me to safety. Then I saw it. A submarine had just emerged, which would now return me to headquarters.

But before I could reach the hatch, Julie, one of the lifeguards at our recreation center, stepped out from behind a pillar. Julie was one of the most ravishing women I had ever seen. She had a face as pure as snow and had light brown hair that flowed down her back like a gentle stream. Her skin was as smooth as a glass marble. Her figure would make any Miss America contestant delirious with envy. Unfortunately, her personality resembled that of a pit bull with a thorn stuck in its paw.

She walked over to me and said, "I saw you jump over that fence."

"Are you sure it was me?" I asked, playing with her.

"Yes," she snapped back.

"I just didn't feel like walking all the way around the gate," I told her. "Have you noticed how hot it is out there?"

"If you jump over the fence, then other kids will start jumping over the fence," she said.

"No one will do that," I told her. Julie would often overcomplicate problems. She enforced the rules at the ranch like a warden at Alcatraz.

"Oh, really?" she said, her eyes fixed behind me. "I can see your friends from here." She stormed into the hall and I turned my head to see what she was talking about. I looked over towards the fence and saw that Dan and T.J. had jumped it. It was like something out a spy novel. T.J. and Dan would start running; then they would dive behind the nearest object. They would pop their heads up to see if anyone was watching, and then they would start the procedure all over again.

"She already saw you guys," I yelled out. Either they did not hear me or they just wanted to get some practice on their spy techniques, because they still remained hidden. I watched in amazement as they dived behind tables, crawled through the grass and hid behind nearby trash cans.

Finally, they got close enough to where Dan whispered behind a bush, "Hey, Ian."

"She already saw you guys," I told them once again.

"How'd she see us?" T.J. asked.

"She's got eyes like an eagle," I said.

Once in the pool hall, Julie made it her top priority to keep the three of us out of trouble. T.J. had to sit out of the pool for fifteen minutes due to playing too roughly in the pool. Dan and I were told we would soon be joining him if we violated the no running rule again. Did she not notice that there were about twenty other kids in the pool?

It was not just one day either. After this incident, the Dragon, as we called her, watched the three of us like hawks. Every time we entered the recreation center, Julie would not let us out of her sight. We were forced to follow every rule. We were coerced into memorizing every regulation. Julie had made known that she reigned supreme over the recreation center, and the three of us could not help but feel extremely perturbed with the inhumane tyrant.

About a week later, the three of us sat in T.J.'s room trying to think of something to do. "We could go play basketball," Dan suggested.

"Nah, we already did that today," I told him.

"We could go climb the mountain," T.J. said.

"It's too hot," I said. Normally, I would love to hike up the mountain, but the heat wave had not yet passed, and to hike up in this temperature was suicidal. We sat in the room with an electric fan pointing toward us, trying to come up with a worthy idea.

"We can go swimming since its so hot," Dan said.

"Even better, we can go down to the pool and rent one of those paddleboats. We've never done that before," I told them. Our recreation center rented out boats that could be taken out on the man-made lake for an hour's worth of time.

"That's a cool idea," T.J. said.

"But what about me?' Dan asked. "They won't let me go." At eleven years old, Dan was not even allowed inside the recreation center without adult supervision. You had to be at least twelve years of age to get in alone.

"We'll just sneak you in," T.J. said.

"How are you gonna do that?" Dan asked.

"We'll think of that when we get over there," I told him.

"I'm not sure about this," Dan said with a worried look on his face.

"Quit being such a baby," T.J. said.

"You know it costs five dollars," Dan said.

"I've got some money," I said.

"And I've got some change," T.J. said. We put our money together and luckily came up with five dollars and seventeen cents.

"What if we get in trouble?" Dan asked

"Don't worry, Dan. Nothing'll happen," I told him as I put the money in my pocket. The three of us left T.J.'s room, grabbed some towels and started to walk down towards the pool. We walked down Catalejo and over to Guajome. From there, we sneaked through the territory that the Jeep Man oversaw, headed through the field and over to the recreation center.

"I sure hope that Dragon Lady isn't here. She'll get us for sure," Dan said as the three of us stood outside the pool hall.

"Me too," T.J. said agreeing with Dan.

I looked at Dan and said, "You just hide out here till T.J. and I call for you."

I faintly heard Dan mutter, "But what about..." but T.J. and I had already entered the door, leaving Dan to fend for himself.

"Look," T.J. said as he pointed to a beautiful feminine figure walking along the pool.

"Dang, it! The Dragon Lady's here!" I said. "Hurry, let's go in the office before she sees us. We turned the corner and walked into the business office of the pool hall, where we found a woman in her mid-forties sitting behind a desk.

"We'd like to rent a paddleboat," I said.

"We'll need to see your pool ID," she said. T.J. and I pulled out the ID that had been issued to everyone that lived in the ranch. "That will be five dollars." I then pulled out my two dollars bills and a pocket full of change and poured it out onto her desk.

"How much is this?" she asked.

"It's five dollars," I said as I began sorting it out and counting it for her. As I began piling up the nickels, Julie walked in with a conceited glare. I gave a disappointed look at T.J.

"What have you guys done?" she asked as she looked at us.

"These two young gentlemen will be renting a paddleboat," the elderly woman said.

"Let's just make sure they're back in one hour," she said, and she gave us a wicked glare as she left the office. With a sigh of relief, I finished counting the money for the woman. They had sent someone down to prepare the paddleboat and told us it would be waiting for us down by the dock.

Once we finished paying, we left the office and I turned to T.J. and whispered, "You go and find Dan. Then meet me over by the boat and we'll sneak him in."

"I won't come out till the coast is clear," T.J. said. I left T.J. as I walked around the corner to where the boats were held. Down the hill, by the lake, there was a small dock where the paddleboats were tied. Next to the dock was one of the male lifeguards, standing at attention and waiting for my arrival. Praying our plan would work, I walked up to him trying not to act too suspicious.

"Are you ready to go?" he asked.

"Not yet. My friend had to go to the bathroom," I said, hoping the man would walk off. Unfortunately, he still stood there, not budging.

"Do you know how to operate this?" he asked.

"Don't worry. I can take her out," I said, trying to give off my best sailor impression. "I've driven one of these puppies before."

"Ok, just be careful out there," he said as he walked off towards the pool hall.

"Will do," I said as I watched him leave. Once the man had gone, T.J. and Dan came around the building and walked down to the lake.

"Dragon lady almost saw me," Dan said.

"Then let's hurry up and get out of here before she does," I said as T.J. and I climbed in the boat, taking up the two seats.

"Hurry up," T.J. said to Dan.

"Sit behind us and stay low so they can't see you," I told him. Dan crawled in behind us and tucked his head below our bodies. T.J. untied the boat and pushed us off. We drifted out, leaving the dock, and T.J. and I began paddling.

"Let's go way out there," T.J. said.

"Yeah, then no one will be able to see us swimming," I said as I continued to steer us away from the recreation center.

"But no one is supposed to go swimming in the lake," Dan said, still curled up in the back.

"That's why were gonna go where no one can see us," I told him. We paddled even farther away from the center and started to reach the middle of the lake.

"This is hard," T.J. said, exhausted from his continuous paddling.

"I know," I answered. "But we gotta keep going until we get there." We paddled on a bit further until I felt satisfied.

"Is that enough?" T.J. asked.

"That should do it," I said. "Are you guys ready to go swimming?"

"You guys go in and I'll join you later," T.J. said.

"I'll think I'll stay on the boat too," Dan said.

"Come on. Look how far away they are," I said. "They can't see us from here."

"I am hot," Dan said as he wiped some sweat from his forehead and looked at the perspiration on his hand.

"Good, then let's hurry up and get out there," I told him. We took off our shirts and shoes and jumped into the lake. The summer heat had become a memory as the exhilarating water instantly soothed our wearied bodies.

"This feels good," Dan said as both of us began treading water.

"Even better than the pool," I told him. For the next couple of minutes, Dan and I splashed each other as we swam around enjoying the water.

I watched as Dan stopped swimming and looked at the boat drifting off. "Where's he going?" Dan asked.

"So long, suckers," T.J. said. I could already sense what T.J. was planning. With his warped way of thinking, he planned on leaving us stranded in the middle of the lake.

"Get back here!" I yelled as I swam after the boat. Although, the paddleboat went slowly, it was still too fast for me to catch it.

"Ian, I can't swim anymore!" an exhausted Dan yelled. I looked back to see Dan splashing frantically in the lake.

"Go to the shore!" I yelled, as I too was fatigued from chasing T.J. We started swimming back and frantically tried to make it to the shore. We conserved no energy as we raced back to the shore. Our arms and legs burned from the intense workout.

"I can't go anymore, Ian!" Dan yelled.

"Just keep going," I told him. We had been swimming for minutes. My lungs gasped for air. The pain was overwhelming. I looked up and saw Dan struggling to make it to the shore. He was closer than I was since I had gone back to chase T.J. Then, an incredible pain surged through my left leg. Of all times to obtain a cramp! The lower half of my body drifted to the bottom while my arms struggled to keep me afloat.

As my body sank into the water, my feet descended into some sort of slimy substance. It was as if I had stepped into a bowl of pudding. My body drifted down until my feet slid through the sludge and touched something hard. I pushed off against it and catapulted myself back to the surface and yelled, "We're at the shore, Dan! We're at the shore!" My good news gave Dan a burst of inspiration as I watched him swim up to the shore. I soon followed as I made it to the shore and fell to the ground. We both lay on the ground coughing and gasping for air.

After Dan had spit out some water, he looked at me and said, "I can't believe we swam that far."

"I know. I thought we weren't gonna make it," I said, still breathing hard as the cramp in my leg began to loosen.

"That was sure stupid of T.J.," Dan said.

"Yeah, where is he?" I asked. I looked out into the lake and saw T.J. and the paddleboat.

"Get over here!" Dan yelled out.

"Why don't you guys swim out here?" T.J. said.

"Just come on!" I yelled out to T.J. T.J. steered the boat over and brought it over to us. He pulled the boat up alongside the shore and we crawled into it.

"What were you thinking?" Dan asked.

"Don't ever do that again. Dan and I barely made it back," I said.

"I was just messin' around," T.J. said.

"You could have killed us out there," Dan said.

"Ok, ok. Sheesh! You guys can't take a joke," he said as we sailed off out into the lake again. It was one of my personal dilemmas. While T.J. would indeed add excitement to our lives, he also brought danger along with it. None of us knew what he was capable of, yet we all feared the coming day when he would go over the edge. I just hoped he would not take any of us with him. While I pondered these thoughts, Dan and

I sat in the boat regaining our strength. Meanwhile, T.J. took us out even further into the lake. We had gone far past the danger buoys that no boats were aloud to pass.

"Let's go over there and light some firecrackers," I said, pointing to some tunnels. In actuality, the tunnels were one huge bridge that led cars over the lake. The tunnel also led to the polluted side of the lake, which was forbidden to all vessels.

"But we're not supposed to go over there," Dan said.

"Just think of all the rules we've already broken," T.J. said.

"And just think of how neat those fireworks will look in that dark tunnel!" I said. T.J. paddled on as we brought the boat up to the edge of the tunnel. There were four passages to choose from. Each took you to the other side of the lake. We opted for the one closest to us and went into the tunnel. As we entered the tunnel, the summer's light faded more and more the further in we went.

Once we were at the middle of the tunnel, I said, "Let's do the fireworks now." T.J. pulled out a small handful of some firecrackers we had been saving from last year's Fourth of July. "Light them on that side of the boat, so they don't burn us." I had burned my thumb before using a firework and I never wanted to experience that pain again. T.J. took out his dad's cigarette lighter from his other pocket. He then lit the firecracker, dropped it and we all ran to the front of the boat.

The fuse shrunk, and in a second, the firecracker quickly lit and jumped off the boat and landed into the water. "That stunk!" T.J. said. "It only stayed on for a second."

"This time, let's put it down in the seats; then it won't be able to get out of the boat," I told them. Dan and I got out of the seats and crawled over to the front of the boat. T.J. pulled out another firecracker, set it down inside the seat, lit the fuse and joined us on the edge of the boat. The three of us gazed down at the fuse and watched in anticipation.

In the next second, the firecracker exploded. It flew around the inside of the boat, bouncing off everything it touched as if it were a drunken firefly. We watched as the firecracker changed the color of the tunnel from its original from damp gray to pink to green and then to yellow. Then as quickly as it started, it died down and the tunnel returned to its original drab color.

"That was so cool!" I said.

"Did you see all the colors?" Dan asked.

"That was just too neat," T.J. said.

"Good thing we weren't near it," I said as I pointed to the inside of the boat. Inside the boat, on the sections where the firecracker had hit, were little black burnt spots.

"I hope they don't see that," Dan said, talking of the pool administration. The three of us got back inside the boat. As I got into my seat, I stared down at the water. It looked deathly eerie. It looked extremely surreal and as black as coffee. Probably no one had ever been dumb enough to get in it before. I had to be the first.

"Let's get in this water," I told Dan.

"Are you crazy? Don't you remember what happened last time we got in?" Dan asked.

"T.J.'s learned his lesson," I said as I shot an intense glare at T.J.

"You don't have to bring that up again," T.J. said.

"What, how you almost killed us?" Dan said angrily.

"Just look at this water, Dan! We gotta go swimming in it," I told him. "We're so far away, they can't see us from in here." Dan gave his reluctant face as I started to take off my shirt again. Once undressed, Dan and I jumped back into the lake. The water in the tunnel was much colder than the water out in the middle of the lake. I watched as my body seemed to disappear in the black liquid. Still mistrustful of T.J., Dan and I hung onto the edge of the boat while T.J. pulled us through the tunnel. We then exited the tunnel on the other side of the lake. This side of the lake was not as clean as the other side of the lake and was closed for repairs. There were a few plants growing in it and we did not stay that long as T.J. turned the boat around and took us back through the tunnel to the unpolluted side of the lake.

Once we emerged on the other side, T.J. took us back towards the middle of the lake. Starting to feel a bit water logged, I pulled myself back into the boat and began to dry myself. Dan, too, became tired of the water, and tried to pull himself into the boat.

"Here, I'll help you," T.J. said as he extended his hand in servitude. T.J. pulled him out of the water, but just as he was about to enter the boat, T.J. pushed him back in.

Dan fell back into the water and once he reached the surface, he yelled, "You jerk!"

I paid little attention to Dan as I mumbled, "We are dead."

"What's wrong?" T.J. asked.

"That," I said as I pointed out in front of me. Coming towards us was one of the recreation's speedboats. It was piloted by a woman while some man sat in the passenger seat. After staring a bit longer, I could see that the pilot was the infamous Dragon Lady.

"Get in the boat! Get in the boat!" I yelled as T.J. quickly pulled Dan into the boat. Our only chance was to see if we could make it to the shore. We would have to abandon the boat and then take off on foot. Then she would never be able to catch us.

Once Dan had entered the boat, I turned and tried to make it towards the shore. We cruised around five miles per hour, as the speedboat quickly over took us. The speedboat pulled in front of us, cutting off our route to escape.

"What was he doing in that lake?" the Dragon Lady yelled.

At the same time, Dan and T.J. yelled out different excuses. "He pushed me in," Dan said.

"He fell in," T.J. yelled.

"I don't want to hear it," she snapped. She pointed at our boat and the man who had been in the passenger seat pulled out a rope and tied our boat onto theirs. The Dragon Lady then started her boat up and towed us back to the docks.

We sat in the boat quietly until Dan broke the silence and whispered, "I told you we were gonna get in trouble."

"I wonder what they're gonna do to us?" I asked.

"Who knows?" T.J. said.

"I think the Dragon only saw Dan in the lake. I don't think she knows about all the other stuff we were doing out there," I told them.

"Then we'd really be in trouble," Dan said.

"So if they ask, only tell them that we were in the lake," I said. We quickly quieted as the Dragon Lady turned off the boat and let us float back to the dock. Once she finished parking, she came back and secured our boat up.

"I want you guys to wait here until I come back," she said as she walked off, keeping an eye on us.

"What's she gonna do?" Dan whispered to me, but before I could answer the Dragon Lady came back carrying a bucket and dragging a water hose out to us.

"I want you guys to wash these paddleboats and when you're finished, the people in the office are waiting to talk to you. Dan and I grabbed some of the towels that were in the bucket and began scrubbing down the boats. Ten minutes had passed before we realized that T.J. had done nothing but hold the hose. And after having him finish up, we started to make our way towards the pool hall.

"Remember, don't tell them anything else we did," I said as we walked up the hill towards the pool hall. We walked inside, into the offices, and found ourselves confronted by the woman who had rented us the boat.

Once inside, she looked at us and said, "So, you guys were swimming in the lake?"

"Yes," I said in a low tone.

"And you guys know you're not supposed to be on the lake?" she asked.

"Yes," I said again.

"And do you know he's not even old enough to ride on the boats?" she asked. We all turned and tried to act ignorant.

"I guess," I said, trying to look innocent. She sat there for a moment, and I could tell she was thinking of a suitable punishment.

"The three of you are banned from using the boats again for a couple of months and you all can expect some phone calls," she said. She then got up from her desk and went into another room.

The three of us walked outside and T.J. said, "That wasn't so bad."

"Yeah, but what about those phone calls?" Dan said. "Once my dad finds out I'm gonna get in a lot of trouble."

"We'll have to go home and take our phones off the hook for the rest of the night. Then, by the next day these people will probably have forgotten about it," I told them.

"Since we're here, d'you want to go in the pool?" T.J. said, not having gotten wet all day.

"Sure," I said, still feeling energetic. We ran over to the pool, took off our shirts and jumped in. We immediately started thromping and splashing each other in the water. Then, the Dragon Lady came over and gave us an intense glare. She had obviously seen enough of us for one day.

"Let's go, guys," Dan said as we got out of the pool. We picked up our clothes and decided to put them on once we were out of the pool hall. Once we were outside the iron gate, we put on our clothes, hopped the fence, and we started to make our way home.

I felt an urge of sympathy for the Dragon Lady. For today, she had sealed her own fate. She had manufactured her own doom. We would extract revenge on her so heavily her great- grandchildren would feel the repercussions. And as we walked home, I giggled to myself as I planned out my revenge against the evil Dragon Lady.

Later that night, as I lay in bed asleep, my nightmare visited me once again. I found myself again lying in the same coffin. This time, as I pushed the lid off, drops of water trickled into the wooden box. Pushing even harder, I struggled to get the top completely off. Then suddenly the top collapsed and a mountain of water now crashed upon me. I quickly sat up in my bed, the watery illusion disappearing. I checked my surroundings, making sure I was in my bed on dry land. It seemed that death was still out there stalking me.

I looked at the clock. It read four twenty-seven. It was almost morning. I decided not to tempt fate and turned on the light. I wiped the sweat off my forehead with the pillowcase and got out of my bed. I picked up a comic book and prepared myself for the long wait that would bring the safety of the light of dawn.

CHAPTER 5

Thoughts

The sun finally began its descent as I made my way up the trail of our mountain. Late afternoons were my favorite time of the summer days. The smoldering heat would finally fade and you would be left with a perfect temperature for the rest of the night.

Frequently, I would come up to the mountain by myself to let out the stress of school or just to meditate about certain subjects. Today was one of those Saturdays when Dan, T.J. and James had all taken off somewhere with their families and I had spent the entire day at my house bored, doing nothing but watching old episodes of The Flintstones and Gilligan's Island. But I could not complain, for I would rather take a long, tedious, dull Saturday than an enslaved day at school. So, once the broiling heat started to subside, I made my way toward our majestic mountain to spend the rest of the afternoon.

Then, as I made it to the end of the mountain trail, I stopped for a second, letting my weary legs get a breather. I was at the exact spot where Dan, T.J., and I always hung out. This was the same place where we had pitched our tent and had eaten lunch the first time we came up here together. I pulled off the backpack I had been wearing and then placed it up on our split boulder. I climbed up, sat next to by backpack and enjoyed being out of my house away from my parents. As dependable as a rooster crowing in the morning, it was certain that on any dull day my parents would see the pain of my boredom, and like salt to an open wound, would give me chore upon chore to fill up my unoccupied time. I giggled to myself as I thought of them searching the house wondering who would clean up the backyard.

I then unzipped my backpack and pulled out a cold can of grape soda. I pulled off the lid and took a long gulp. While drinking, I stared out in front of me and admired the view. As many times as I had come up to the mountain, the view seemed more awe-inspiring each time. From here I could almost see all of Moreno Valley. I could see our lake and the recreation center; I could see our neighborhood, the school and even the Jeep Man's territory.

And as I tried to take in the vast view I could not help but admire the red radiance filling the sky. Its glare covered the city. It appeared so powerful, seeming to have no bounds, yet at the same time it seemed pure and gentle, filling me with a sense of peace. Minutes passed away like seconds as I gazed at the red jewel in the sky. A smile grew on my face, for this treasure belonged only to me. Only I was deserving of this natural wonder.

Ordinary people were too busy to take notice of this natural gem. Too busy going to work, too busy worrying about financial problems, these mindless people noticed nothing of what was truly going on around them. And as I stared at the sky, I realized I was above them all. I was above all their meaningless problems. I was above their slave-like mentality.

I stared at the ground and looked at the realm below me. The mountain, like myself, lived in a world all its own. I pulled off a tiny leaf of a nearby plant. The green leaf had hundreds of lines running through it, each line heading off in an its own direction. I started to count the tiny lines when my eyes began to strain. I dropped the leaf on the ground and searched for more interesting data.

I then scooped up some sand and began to probe it. The sand was actually made up from tiny microscopic rocks. I looked at the split boulder and noticed the areas that had begun to erode. The sand in my hand matched the eroded sand from the boulder. It began to boggle my mind as I began to wonder how many of these tiny rocks it took to make this whole mountain. I poured the sand out of my hand and wiped the dust onto my shirt.

I began to look at an army of red ants that were crawling around by the leaf I had dropped. I got off the boulder and crawled on all fours so that I could get a better look at them. The ants were amazing. They were as detailed and complicated as the leaf and the pile of sand. They had tiny legs with tiny bodies, which had even smaller heads attached to the body. I giggled as I watched their antennas wiggle around on their heads.

I looked back towards the strawberry sunset. As remarkable as it was, the leaf, the sand and the ants were just as spectacular in their own way. The world itself was amazing.

I wondered why no one else noticed this splendor that engulfed us. For so long, I had known I was different from the average person. I thought differently. I acted differently. I rejected conformity and chose to live in my own world. When I was younger, I thought I was abnormal. I thought there was something I was missing. I though that I was lacking something that made me less of a person. But now, having chosen to never grow up, I realized that it was the world that was lacking something.

How could they go about their daily lives and not notice the beauty that was about them? How could they not partake in the adventures that life had placed for them?

I stared back down at the ants, hoping to gain more great insights, when an astounding idea occurred to me. I watched the ants as they scrambled across the ground. It seemed that all they cared about was getting to their destination. They never even gave a thought to where they were. Some were even in such a hurry that they would crawl over one another in order to get there. They were not even aware that I was there. With one thumb, I could easily squash four or five of them, yet they were unaware to my presence. Death could be only a matter of seconds away and they would not even realize it. The thought was a little chilling.

From atop the hill, I looked down at the streets below. In an uncanny resemblance the cars reminded me of the ants. They scurried around from place to place, only caring about where they were going. I pitied the people down below. These people were unaware of what was really going on around them. Did these people know that death was out there hunting and stalking each one of them? I knew I would be trying to find the cure of death some way, but how could these people go about their daily life with death hanging over their head? It was as if they did not realize how short the time is before we actually die.

"I am so lucky," I whispered to myself. And I was, for I thought things that people don't normally think about and I did things that normal people don't do. I was so glad I was not like the kids my age. While other kids my age were hassling themselves with problems of parties and girlfriends, I was out searching for challenging experiences and exciting quests. These kids who concerned themselves with such insignificant ordeals were wasting their youth. I, on the other hand, had spine-tingling adventures in my future.

I smiled to myself as I thought of how just a few days ago we had barely escaped the Jeep Man. Dan, T.J. and I were in the Jeep Man's territory, with him inches behind us. We had purposely been badgering him during the morning, and finally, he had had enough. He came out of his hut and brought his mechanical beast to life. Unfortunately for us, we had miscalculated the distance between ourselves and the school fence, which held our freedom. His engine thundered behind us, as seconds were the only obstacle that prolonged our capture. But luckily, the Jeep Man had not seen some new wood that had been left by some of the construction workers.

The tiny obstacle bought us enough time as the Jeep Man swerved around the stack of wood while we hopped over it and made our escape.

My face wore a devilish smirk - the grin a retired general has when thinking of hard- fought battles in his past. We had had so many great battles. Life had dealt me a lucky card, for I had live in the most exciting neighborhood in the world. It was a neighborhood where excitement was as plentiful as the stars in the sky.

I recalled the incident when Dan and I got to work with the police on a momentous case by lending them our cunning detective skills. The family two houses down from mine had called the police in regard to an exhibitionist who was loose in our neighborhood. It seems while their two younger daughters were walking down Catalejo street, some man opened his house door, dropped his pants and exposed himself to them. Being only seven and nine, the girls were mortified and ran home and told their parents. Hearing this, Dan and I hopped on our bikes to scope out the pervert and the scene of the crime.

But when we got there, we could not see him. He must have barricaded himself inside. So, while I was in the area, I decided to go visit the kid across the street to see if I could negotiate some deals regarding some priceless baseball cards. Dan and I crossed the street, laid our bikes in his grass and knocked on his door.

After he opened the door and let us in, we quickly went to his room so we could be free to loudly debate the outrageous pricing of some of his cards. Trading cards was an intense ordeal.. We yelled, we screamed, we ranted, trying to find the best trade. After a vehement twenty minutes, we sat in the middle of his room recuperating.

And while we were taking a breather, I said, "Did you hear what happened to Katie and Anna? Some weird guy took off his pants and showed himself to them."

"No way," the baseball card junkie said.

Dan put down a Tony Gwynn and said, "Yah, that's why we came up here."

"He lives right across the street from you guys," I said since Dan had left out that vital piece of information. "The cops are there talking to 'em right now."

"Hey, my mom's been having problems with that guy," he told us as he ran out of his room. He promptly returned with his mom.

She looked at Dan and me and said, "So what happened?" I told her the entire ordeal of the two girls. She then said, "Yah, that creep has been bothering me too. When my husband's gone at work he'll flash a mirror at us through our house. And then sometimes when we're outside he'll just stare at us."

"Really?" I asked in amazement. "Come on, Dan. We gotta go tell the cops!" Dan and I left their house, got back on our bikes and raced down the street. It would appear the years of reading detective comics had finally paid off.

As we turned the corner and headed down Guajome, I could see the two policemen walking toward their car. "Hurry up, they're gettin ready to leave," I told Dan, who was lagging behind a bit.

As the men in uniform approached their car, I said, "Um, we were just talking to this lady, and that weird guy was doing stuff to her too." Both men walked up to us, and Dan I then told them everything that the kid's mom had told us.

"Where does this lady live?" one of the men asked us.

"Up the street," Dan replied.

"We can show you the way," I said eagerly. The men agreed and they both opened their doors to get in the car. "Hey, can I get in the back?" I asked, hoping one of my fantasies would be fulfilled.

The cop smiled and replied, "Nope." He was probably too jealous that I would take the credit for this collar. So Dan and I saddled up once again, and with thoughts of Dan and me busting down the lunatic's door, we led the police car to the kid's house. On that account, the kid's mom ended up giving her statement to the police, but Dan and I left before we got to see the outcome since we were already late for our lunch.

We had encountered so many eerie experiences in our neighborhood. I had already forgotten some of our past adventures; my mind tended to focus on the adventure at the present moment while forgetting the events of yesterday. I might have to start writing some of them down so I would not forget any more. But I could sense that there was something about this neighborhood, something that would help me in my war against death. I had not progressed much in my morbid quest since my nightmares, yet I felt as if I were traveling down the right path.

The conquest of Lady Death had something to do with not growing up. I was positive of this fact. Once you chose to grow up, to take the steps towards adulthood, your fate was ultimately doomed. You would not be able to turn back and reclaim your childhood.

Although I had taken the right course in my search for the deathly cure, I was uncertain of what to do next. Where was I to go from here? I was trying to solve a riddle that had perplexed mankind since Adam and Eve first walked the earth. I felt as if the road I was traveling on was coming to a fork, and the trail I chose would decide my destiny. But was I deluding myself? How could I possibly stop death? Could a fifteen-year-old boy succeed where great philosophers and thinkers had failed? This was my destiny though, as I tried to erase the doubts from my mind. Death probably had figured I was on her trail and was trying to cloud my mind with doubts and skepticism. Perhaps my age was the perfect weapon. My youthful experience could lead me to triumph where the ancient one's decrepit wisdom was their downfall.

I glanced down at my watch to see if it was time for me to return home. I watched in curiosity as the seconds rolled away effortlessly. Then as the seconds began to pass, the minute hand moved up a notch. A minute had advanced and I could not go back and change it. I now watched in horror as I watched the seconds move until the minute changed once again. I was now one minute closer to death. What I did in that last minute was permanently cemented, written in the great book of history.

I deduced that death had a hidden ally, an ally that I had not foreseen. This was another veiled enemy, who aligned with death formed an unbeatable team - the only person death needed to carry out its fatal duties. Sitting up on the boulder watching the red gleam in the sky I knew that another villain had been added to my rogues gallery. I realized that while I sat, seconds passed away never to return and that this atrocity was happening continuously.

This changed everything. What I did yesterday had been erased forever. What I had done a week ago was nothing more than a memory. I wanted to take my watch off and hurl it down the mountain. But my watch was just an ignorant pawn of father time. I took a deep breath, realizing that there would never be a yesterday again. I was fifteen years old, yet how did fifteen years of my life cruise by without me noticing? I looked at my watch again and noticed that the minute had changed again. Time was moving without my knowledge. No enemy is more treacherous than the kind who hides, waiting to unsuspectingly ambush you in your moment of weakness.

And with this enemy, I could get no help from Dan or T.J. I was truly on my own with this one. At least with the Jeep Man or Dragon Lady, I could see what they were up to. Death and time ambushed you so quickly, that before you realized what either of them were up to it was already to late. You would find yourself spending your last few minutes in some foster home eating mashed potatoes while death waited outside your door.

My mind began to ease as I wondered what time could do against a boy who pledged to never grow up. And although I had not been noticing time, at least, I had been making the most of it. I was living the way I wanted to live. I was doing the things I wanted to do. I may have let some days slip away without my notice, but I was more aware now. I knew how precious the world was and how sacred the time we have was.

And while death had a powerful ally, I too had a mighty comrade. Our mountain had mystical attributes that were available to me. One was that it seemed to bring about deep introspection. It unearthed great thoughts from me and challenged me in ways that no school test ever could. If there was any solution to this death equation, I knew I could solve it at this mountain.

As confident and confused about death as I was before, I laid back on the split boulder and gazed into the heavens above me. Death was still at large, but I knew I would defeat it, for I was Ian Ramos, the greatest boy adventurer of all time. So, with a breeze blowing by and soothing my body, I stared at the stars and wondered why I had never noticed how beautiful God created the stars.

CHAPTER 6

Max

Our summer had faded into long memories while the dreaded school year was now upon us. School represented everything that I loathed about life. School was just a more moderate form of slavery. Every morning we were dragged out of bed at some inhuman time, so we could shower and dress, and then we were led like cattle to some deplorable labor camp site where we would carry out moronic rituals until the bell at three o'clock sounded our freedom. We then had to repeat this five times until the weekend, which lasted only two measly days. Why did some uptight adults have the right to take away my freedom? School must have been invented by some barbaric conquerors who forced the kids of the enslaved country into agonizing labor camps. Then somehow, the slaves must of grown accustomed to it, and then passed the horrible tradition down to each generation.

I despised everything concerning school, from the idiotic rules of "no chewing gum on campus" to the boring lectures our Spanish teacher Mrs. Davis would give on pronunciation. With the passing of each school day, a small portion of my childhood spirit was being torn away. How ironic that in a locality where kids gathered, we were being brainwashed to stop acting juvenile and were being prepared for the dismal adult world.

While most of the students sat in class taking notes on the lecture like trained seals, I dreamed of exploring the mountain, searching for the mythical mountain lion, playing See 'n Seek and battling with the Jeep Man. I did not belong in school any more than Tarzan would in Beverly Hills. Simply put, the burden of school, grades and homework left me feeling drained and depressed.

One tedious school night, I lay on my living room carpet trying to figure out the hypotenuse theorem so that I might be able to complete my math homework. I munched on tortilla chips and sipped on orange soda as I flipped the channels on the television set. I dropped my pencil in frustration, slammed my book and lay back on the carpet. I was filled to the brim with utter boredom. I longed for a quick excursion to the mountain. If there was anything that could take away my school-time depression, it would be the mountain. I began to wonder about the mysterious caves that might be hidden somewhere in the mountain.

Earlier one night, I had seen some bats flying around the lampposts. I knew bats took up dormancy in caves and the nearest place where a cave could be located had to be somewhere up in the mountain. I would have to call the guys together one day, so we could spread out and start searching the mountain. I could make some diagrams and maps of the mountain so I could plot out some of the more likely spots where the cave could be hidden. Our expeditions would probably take weeks or months, and could only be done during the summer. But for now, I could plan, as I tried scanning the mountain in my mind. But my mental surveys were broken up when a tremendous pounding noise rang through my house. The resounding sound could only mean that T.J. was knocking on the door. I stood up, walked over to the door and peered through the window. Sure enough, it was T.J.

I opened the door, and then T.J. asked, "Hey, Ian. Can you come outside?"

"I've got homework to do, but I'll come outside for a couple of minutes," I said as I joined him outside. "So what have you been up to?"

T.J. set his skateboard down, looked at me enthusiastically, and said, "I thought of a great idea for See 'n Seek. I'm gonna make masks for us out of some black T-shirts.

That way it will be even harder to see us." See 'n Seek was the neighborhood game that T.J. and I had invented. It was our own version of hide and seek, but instead of tagging someone you just had to locate the hidden person. We would all dress in black or dark clothes and wait until the sun fell. Then we would start the game. You could hide anywhere. We hid on rooftops, under cars, inside trash cans; any place you could find was legal. There were no boundaries either. T.J. had even been chased out of someone's yard from a man with a gun.

"That's cool, we'll look like ninjas," I said. "But won't your mom care that you're cutting up your shirts?"

"Naw, they're old shirt and plus, she won't care anyway," T.J. said. Hopefully, this wouldn't turn out to be like the time T.J., his brothers, Dan and I played See 'n Seek in the unfinished houses. T.J.'s mom found out, and out of anger came down and drove his brothers home while T.J. hid in the port-o-potty. Ever since I met him, T.J. had always been a poor judge concerning things his mother cared about.

We walked around the side of the house planning the next game when we noticed a sparkle in the autumn night. "What the heck is that?" I asked T.J.

"I don't know. Let's go find out," T.J. said.

We tiptoed over to the sparkle and saw a familiar form. The sparkle turned out to be the eyes of my next door neighbor's dog. "Hey, that's Max," I told T.J. Max was an extremely massive pure bred German shepherd, but he was as gentle as a butterfly.

T.J. looked at him and asked, "What's he doin' out here?"

"He must've gotten out somehow. Come on. Let's go put him back in," I said, wanting to put the gigantic dog in its backyard before it decided to run away from home.

We walked over to Max and T.J. reached out his hand trying to grab hold of Max's collar. In a flash, Max snapped at

T.J.'s hand. Luckily T.J. yanked his hand back, saving his fingers and himself from being nicknamed stumpy. Max stood up snarling and bearing his fangs for T.J. and myself to see. We began to creep backwards as I tried to calm Max down by repeatedly saying in a soothing voice, "Down boy. Down boy." The volume of Max's growl escalated while a drop of saliva dripped from his mouth onto the cement. He then started barking rapidly while he walked towards us.

I had heard of dogs being driven insane, foaming at the mouth and visciously attacking people who had once befriended them. I had not detected any foam on Max, but in any event, we were now facing a deranged dog.

"Man, is he mad!" T.J. said in a worried voice. "I think we're in big trouble."

"Just don't make any sudden moves," I told him, wishing I had gone up to the mountain instead of staying home and doing my homework. We trembled at the sight of the enraged beast coming closer to us. "I think he's gettin' ready to come get us," I said as I made a mental reference of an animal show where the lion attacked its prey.

"On the count of three, let's run into your house," T.J. said as we continued to slowly creep backwards. Running from an angry dog had to be one of the most ludicrous acts you could do, but our time was running out, leaving me with no other options.

"O.k., I whispered to T.J. as if Max could hear.

"One," T.J. said as the snarling Max came closer.

I cleared my throat, feeling like a man who was about to go sky diving, and slowly said, "Two."

T.J. and I glanced at each other and simultaneously said, "Three." We turned, screamed and sprinted toward my front door. I looked behind and saw Max making his charge. Using his hind legs, he sprung forth like a rattlesnake leaping at its victim. I could hear Max's paws hitting the pavement as he gained on us.

The front door was just a few feet from us, but so was Max. I ran as fast as I could. The only thoughts I had were making it to the door. I could hear Max getting closer as I reached my hand out towards the doorknob. I grabbed it, turned it, opened the door and ran in. I looked to see Max a few feet away from T.J. T.J. dove into the doorway. I took one final stare at Max and then I slammed the door, nearly striking Max's face.

"Now that was close," I said to T.J.

"How close was he behind me?" T.J. asked.

"You don't want to know," I told him.

"Let's see where he is," T.J. said. We walked over to the window and looked through it. Max just walked around the side of the house until he disappeared around the garage.

"Looks like he's gone for now," I said.

"Let me go call my mom and tell her that I'll be over here for a while," T.J. said as he walked over to use my phone. This was not going to sit well with my dad. He had always thought of T.J. as a troublemaker and did not like him hanging around the house. It would definitely be best if I could get T.J. out of the house by the time my dad got home.

I joined T.J. in the living room, where he had finished making his phone call and was now watching television. "What'd your mom say?" I asked.

"She said she'd come get me in a while," he told me. Knowing T.J., this probably meant five hours from now. After watching TV with him for the next thirty minutes, I saw no sign of his mom coming to pick him up.

"You know Max is probably gone by now," I said to T.J.

"Maybe," he said as his concentration was focused on the television.

"I'll go check," I said as I got up and walked towards the front door. I peeked out the window and saw no sign of Max. The view, though, did not give me the whole picture. He could be anywhere outside, and I could not send T.J. home with Max lurking about. I opened the door and slowly walked outside.

I walked around the side of my house over to my driveway. I did not see any trace of Max. I looked into my neighbor's yard. Jennifer, Max's owner, had not returned home yet. Max still had to be outside. I walked out into the middle of the street to get a better view. I still saw no sign of Max. I looked up and down Guajome and found nothing. Perhaps he had run out of the neighborhood.

I started to turn around, so I could go back in the house. I would have him home before my dad knew that he had set foot in the house. As I began to walk back, I noticed a sparkle in the air. I walked up closer to it. I gasped in terror as the sparkle turned out to be the light reflecting off Max's eyes.

On the side of me, Max now blocked the way back home. He stood up and started growling as he made his way over towards me. I began to grow very scared as I wished I could call out to T.J. for help. I walked back slowly, hoping Max would forget about me and move on. I had no such luck. Max began jogging a little closer.

My legs shook as Max had now forced me into the neighbors' yard across the street from mine. The house sat in between Dan's and James' houses. Hopefully, one of them would see me and come out to assist me. As I walked up their driveway, Max started barking like some mad dog. Had a rabid raccoon bit him? He was acting uncontrollable.

Max came closer to me as it looked as if he was ready to pounce upon me. Down the street, a car pulled out of the driveway preparing to leave its house. Max turned around and watched the car drive off. With Max's head turned, I kneeled down and picked up a rock in case I needed a weapon.

I figured this distraction would be my only chance to make it out safely. I ran to my neighbor's door and banged on it with my fist. No one came to the door. Fearing Max would soon forget the car; I hid behind a nearby pillar. I peeked around the side of the pillar and saw Max jogging this way. I was not sure if Max knew where I was or not, but I was not going to wait and find out.

I lifted the rock into the air. I gazed at my target. I threw the rock and watched it hit its mark. The rock landed in some nearby bushes and made a loud rustling noise. Max sprinted over to it and began barking at the bush. Using this opportunity, I sprinted across the street.

Without turning my head to see where Max was, I ran across the street, through my front yard and then inside my house. T.J. walked up to find me by the front door breathing heavily. "What have you been doing?" he asked.

"I was outside and Max almost got me," I said.

"Where is he now?" T.J. asked.

"He's still out there somewhere," I said. Peering out the window for a couple of minutes, we saw no sign of Max. We went upstairs to my computer and started to play some video games. Every now and then, I would peek out the window and see if Jennifer had returned home yet.

Another thirty minutes had passed when I checked the window. However, this time I could see that Jennifer was now home. Parked in her driveway was their black Ford truck. "Hey, Jen's home," I told T.J. We turned off the computer, walked downstairs and then headed outside. We walked around the corner of my house, to see Max being held by his collar by Jennifer.

"Finally, you guys got home," T.J. said.

"You won't believe all the trouble Max had caused," I said.

"Yeah, he..." T.J. said as his sentence was broken up by Max's wild barking. It would seem the very sight of us drove Max insane. Max broke free of Jen's grip. He sprinted towards me. I stood frozen. He bared his teeth and my eyes seemed to focus on his fangs. I closed my eyes and prepared for the worst. Was this it? Was I going to die? I put my hands in front of my head, hoping to shield my face.

With my eyes closed, I felt the patter of paws coming towards me and then felt a brush of hair rustle against me. I opened my eyes to see that Max had run right past me. He was not pursuing me but T.J. Max charged T.J., but T.J. swung his skateboard at the beast, coming within inches of hitting its nose. The beast lunged again, but T.J. swung back and again narrowly missed the dog's face. Max stopped lunging at T.J. and backed off as T.J. continued swinging his board.

Laura came up from behind Max, grabbed his collar and said, "Bad dog." She dragged him over to her yard and put him in the fence.

"That was close," I said to T.J.

"I know. I thought I was dead," he said.

"You probably would have been if you didn't swing your board like that," I said.

"I know," T.J. said as he looked down at his watch.

"What is it?" I asked.

"I'd better get home," he said.

"Well, if you gotta go," I said. "I'll see ya tomorrow." I watched T.J. walk off a little bit and then returned inside and started doing my homework.

Through the next day and the following week, I told everyone of our adventure with the savage beast. I told them how we barely escaped this insane creature. I told of how Max was the strongest, fiercest dog in the world.

The next Saturday, I stood in my driveway replaying the events for a kid named Thomas. He was not as impressed with the story as the others had been. "Are you kidding me?" he asked.

"No, it's the truth," I said.

"That dog doesn't look so tough," he said as he looked at Max. Max lay in the neighbors' front yard, chained to a pole that had been lodged in the ground.

"Trust me. That's not a dog you want to mess with," I warned.

"Aw, he's not so scary," he said. "Watch this."

"I wouldn't do anything," I said. Thomas ignored my words as he ran over to Max and began taunting him.

"Wake up," he yelled loudly in Max's ear. Max opened his eyes and stared at him. "Come on. Try and get me!" Thomas began running back and forth trying to stir Max up.

His plan was working. Max stood up and began barking. "Did I make you mad?" he taunted the dog as he danced in front of it.

"You better stop!" I yelled.

But he did no such thing as he kept yelling and teasing the dog. "Try and get me. Try and get me," he yelled. Then, it was as if Max suddenly understood English. The dog charged towards Thomas. Thomas stood vainly away at a good distance as he watched the dog race forward. Then, as the chain tightened up, the pole, which was lodged into the ground, flew up into the air. Thomas turned in horror as he tried to run. I watched in amazement as Max leaped onto Thomas' back. Thomas screamed aloud.

"Get on top of the car," I yelled. Once Max fell off Thomas' back, Thomas immediately jumped and climbed up top of my mother's Mazda RX7. Max jumped up and down as he snapped at his feet. Thomas lay huddled in the middle of the roof trying to stay as far away from the dog as possible.

Fortunately for Thomas, Joe, Jennifer's dad, came outside and pulled Max back into the backyard. Once Max was at a safe distance away, Thomas got down from the car, lifted his shirt up and said, "Look where it got me." On his back there were two bumps the size of grapes.

"I tried to warn you," I said as I walked the frightened boy home. As Joe put Max back inside, I caught a final glimpse of the magnificent beast. He was a worthy opponent who I knew I would come across again someday.

CHAPTER 7

Reunion with the Jeep Man

"It's all back," I thought to myself as T.J. and I walked down the street. The kids waiting on the corner for the ice cream truck to drive by. The June bugs flying around pulling 360's while narrowly missing objects. The cloudless skies that hung around and made you forget the notion of the term "bad weather." All of this and more had returned. With only a week left of school, it was a time of joyous celebration and kind treatment to thy fellow man, for summer had returned.

And with the rebirth of summer came the end of an agonizing school sentence. It was quite peculiar. Another school year had passed and I had felt no more intelligent than the year before. I was just as certain as I was last year that I never wanted to return to that accursed hell- whole. My school year had been filled with torturous homework assignments, grades that barely passed and some that didn't, and days where I would have to pick up garbage from the lunch area due to some mischief I had gotten myself into. But those incidents were now unpleasant memories that were better left not thought about.

But other than a depressing school year, we had also been dealt some major changes. First of all, Dan had moved away. Dan's family now lived in a bigger house that they owned instead of renting. Luckily, he had only moved down a couple of streets. In fact, he still lived in the neighborhood and the ranch. It would take about a good five-minute walk to get to his house. It wasn't the same as him living across the street, but it was bearable.

He now lived on the other side of the Jeep Man's territory, across the street from the school that we used as a haven from the Jeep Man. Of course, now you could never be too cautious when going to Dan's house, for fear of a surprise jeep attack, but as long as he lived in walking distance I was content.

Second, with Dan's moving came new adventures, new foes, and new friends. The most significant of those would be Harold. He lived over by Dan across the street from the school. He was the first "other" black kid who had moved in that we had met. He was a scrawny twelve year old, about Dan's height, but still not as frail as Dan. We had met him at Victoriano while playing basketball. Harold came by walking his dogs. We petted his dogs, conversed with him, and after that day Harold became inseparable from the rest of us.

Of course, this was not by our choice. After weeks of hanging around, we had all unearthed Harold's most annoying flaw. He was a compulsive liar. Our first hint came when Harold had told Dan of how he could run the mile clocked somewhere underneath two minutes. This was pretty amazing seeing that the Olympic record is three minutes and thirty two seconds and is held by Sebastion Coe. Then, Harold told me how he could bench press two hundred pounds. This too was amazing considering he was a twelve year old who needed help climbing a fence.

All of the gang would become extremely frustrated with Harold and at times wondered why we bothered keeping him around. But despite all the unbelievable whoppers, deep down we liked Harold. I was probably at the top of the "Save Harold" fan club, for he would sit and eagerly listen with wonder as I told him of our adventurous tales. Then, unlike most twelve year olds, he would become extremely excited and begged to take part in our next scheme. This was the first person I had met who wanted to participate in our adventures simply to partake in the adventure. The others had their own reasons for coming along. T.J. came because we were causing some kind of trouble. James came just to follow the group, and Dan came only because I would force him to. It was refreshing to meet someone with a good taste for adventure.

And if Dan's moving and Harold's arrival weren't big enough, there was the falling of grace of our companion. For so long, T.J. had been walking the tight rope with the neighborhood. But over time, parents began to get fed up with him. Stories of fights, bullying kids and smoking and drinking ran rampant throughout the neighborhood. Some were not true, yet some were. T.J. was slipping toward the path of no redemption. He was more prone to dangerous outbursts and chose to settle disputes with threats or violence. More parents began forbidding their kids to hang around T.J., and unfortunately my overbearing father had hopped onto the bandwagon.

I was not allowed to go over to T.J.'s house. I was not allowed to go places with T.J. and I was not allowed to even be seen with T.J. Of course, I would not let my Dad's threats keep me away from one of my closest friends. I just had to be a little sneakier when hanging out with T.J.

But although being forbidden to see T.J. was depressing, what kept my mind preoccupied was my growing obsession with death. I had learned vital information for my holy crusade. Death and time were linked. They were allies that used each other for their needs.

With this info, I was a little closer to my final victory but still far from my ultimate goal. There were still many sleepless nights with nightmares and morbid visions of my untimely demise. Would possessing eternal youth still be enough to defeat death? I remained positive that it would, yet at the same time death still extremely frightened me. But now it was summer again, and like a child who turns on the light to chase the terror of the dark away, I too had the light of summer protecting me.

And on this summer day, T.J. and I left Dan's new house and began to head home. We crossed the street, walked through the school yard, and then hopped over the fence into the construction area otherwise known as Jeep Man territory. Having to walk through the Jeep Man's territory every time we were going to or leaving Dan's house was a major drag. I guess it was just one of those perks of having your best friend live on the other side of your archenemy.

As we walked over some piles of plywood, we reminisced over last year's summer.

"I'm so glad we're almost out of school," T.J. said. "I was getting sick of that place." T.J. scratched his head with the cast on his arm. T.J. had broken his arm about a week ago in a fierce basketball game at school. It was not too serious though. The cast was supposed to come off in a couple of weeks.

"I know, me too. And we're gonna have so much fun this summer!" I told T.J.

"Man, last summer sure was fun," T.J. said.

"This summer will be even better," I told him. "I've got tons of good ideas for us." I had spent many school days locked behind a desk daydreaming of future summer adventures. Those days seemed to roll by like molasses, but now my summer was here. I giggled to myself as I thought of the moronic teachers who would soon be left behind.

"You know who we haven't seen in a long time?" T.J. asked as he looked over to the purple trailer.

"Jeep man," I said, finishing his thought. And T.J. was correct; mostly due to school and extracurricular activities, we had hardly seen the Jeep Man recently. "Now, that's what makes a summer good," I said, referring to our ordeals with the Jeep Man.

We both looked at each other with mischievous grins. T.J. then giggled and asked, "So do ya wanna?

"Let's do it," I said, as we turned around and made our way back towards the construction area. Once we reached the construction area, I gazed upon the Jeep Man's timeless fortress. Like a sacred monument, it had stood there for years, symbolizing the law and order of our neighborhood. Looking upon the magnificent trailer instantly swept me away with memories of daring chases and narrow getaways. In fact, some of those getaways had been a little too narrow. Some of those escapes were not due to my sheer scheming, but blind luck. With so many brushes with the Jeep Man, did we really want to tempt fate again? But I brushed my worries aside as I remembered who I was. I was Ian Ramos. I was the boy who would someday defeat death. With that in my head, I gritted my teeth and prepared for battle.

T.J. looked over and asked, "You ready?"

"Yah," I said, giving T.J. the green light to proceed. T.J. then took a step forward and gave the trailer a peculiar, evil glare.

He scratched the top of his head and then yelled, "Hey, Jeep Man. We're back. Get your butt out here and get us if you can." We waited the traditional couple of seconds to let the Jeep Man finish whatever it was he was doing in there. I imagined he spent his time going over maps of the neighborhood, discussing his future plots and strategies and jotting down ideas on his future reign of the neighborhood. Not waiting any longer, T.J. yelled out, "Hurry up and come out here and get us."

Still, there was no movement. This did not faze us though. Due to past dealings, we knew that sometimes the Jeep Man would take minutes before he came out of his den. T.J. started to yell, "Hey jeep..." but had not finished his sentence when the door flew open. Our arch nemesis stood in the doorway giving us that familiar glare. No matter how many confrontations we had had the Jeep Man, the effect of his glare was as cold and powerful as it was on our first meeting.

"Let's go," I mumbled to T.J., hoping we could get a well needed head start. We turned and started running away in the opposite direction. We sprinted hard, trying to put as much distance as we could between the Jeep Man and ourselves. Our neighborhood pastime with the Jeep Man was going to become a lot tougher.

Due to further construction, the Jeep Man's trailer had been relocated. It still was in the construction area, but now it lay along the fence of the school. We could no longer take the easy route when running from the Jeep Man. We could no longer hop over the school fence and bathe in the safety and security it gave us. Perhaps the Jeep Man had intentionally designed this or perhaps it had just been our bad luck. Either way, the Jeep Man now had a major advantage.

We sprinted away, leaving the school and the construction area behind us. We crossed the street, wondering where we would run to. As I pondered our next move, I became frightened, and not with the usual fear the Jeep Man dispensed. This time was different. Before, I had some sense of a plan. The Jeep Man would chase us; we'd run, hop the fence and be safe. Now, I had no idea where we were going.

I could hear the Jeep Man slam the door of his jeep. Maybe I should have thought this out a little bit more. I then heard the Jeep Man's engine roar to life. The main wall was about a half mile away and the Jeep Man only needed a few seconds to apprehend us. We sprinted down the street looking for some route that would take us to safety.

"What are we going to do?" T.J. asked frantically. I said nothing while I searched my mind for answers. I turned my head to see the Jeep Man pull his car around and began barreling toward us. The main wall was the safest haven, but the path to get there was too wide open. There was nothing but open land, and with nothing to hide behind, the Jeep Man would surely nab us. Our only chance was to make it to my house.

With the Jeep Man right behind us, I yelled out, "This way!" We made a sharp right and headed toward some of the unfinished houses. Alongside of us were houses that the construction workers had not yet completed. They stood there with the cement laid out and the foundation up, but with no walls. We ran through what would some day be a garage, sprinted through a future living room and jumped out of a soon to be window into their backyard.

The Jeep Man now would have to drive around the houses to get us. The shortcut we had taken would save us time but not our lives. The Jeep Man's detour at best gave us about twenty more seconds of freedom, not to mention that the fact that we had ran through the unfinished houses had surely angered the Jeep Man. Of all the Jeep Man's duties, his first obligation was to keep the kids away from the houses that still needed much more work. We had now given the Jeep Man a legitimate reason to throw us in jail.

Once we were out of the backyard, we sprinted across the street to some of the recently completed houses. We then ran down the street, and then around the corner house where I could now see my backyard. The only problem was that it was too far away. From where we stood, it'd take a couple of minutes before we could reach it, and from the sound of the Jeep Man, we only had a few seconds before he was on us. To make matters worse, there was nothing but a clear path between my backyard and us. With no obstacles to hide behind or dodge, the Jeep Man would catch us in a second. The time we had gained by running through the houses was quickly dwindling.

"What are we gonna do?" T.J. asked frantically.

"I don't know," I told him. "Hide somewhere!" We scrambled around trying to find any object to hide behind. We could hear a loud roaring engine coming down the street. We both knew it was the Jeep Man. The Jeep Man was coming for us and we were standing around like helpless toddlers. I breathed heavily as I searched frantically for somewhere to hide.

I spotted a large chunk of grass nearby. I quickly lay down in the patch, but the grass did not come close to covering me. A few feet away from me, T.J. was trying to position himself behind a rock, but he fared no better than I did. The rock did not even fully cover his face let alone the rest of his body.

The sound of the Jeep Man's engine was growing alarmingly loud. I could tell the Jeep Man was right around the corner. It would seem we had played Russian roulette with the Jeep Man too many times. My heart beat loudly as I feared the inevitable. Would the Jeep Man tar and feather us? Would he lock us in his trailer and leave us to rot? It seemed we would soon find out. But just as I was about to throw in the towel, my basic instincts took over. Without thinking, I ran up to the corner house, hopped the fence and landed in someone's backyard.

"I did it," I gasped to myself. Luckily, the owners of the house appeared not to be home as I noticed all the curtains were drawn down. But in my hasty action, I had forgotten about T.J. He was trapped on the side with the Jeep Man. With his cast on, he had no way of joining me in the backyard. I peeked through one of the cracks on the wood to take a look at T.J.'s situation. But as I looked through, T.J. flipped himself over the fence and landed hard on the ground, almost breaking his other arm. It was one of the most amazing feats I had ever witnessed. T.J., using only one hand, had managed to flip himself over a five feet tall fence. But we did not have time to marvel at the amazing act. I quickly looked through a nearby knot in the fence and saw the Jeep Man race by. We had miraculously done it again. Another spectacular escape from the Jeep Man!

"We did it!" I told T.J. enthusiastically as I pulled away from the hole.

"Where is he?" T.J. asked, still sitting on the ground from his fall.

"He drove by," I told him.

"He didn't even see us?" T.J. asked.

"Nope, he went right by," I said. "And how did you get over that fence?"

"I'm not sure. I just did," T.J. said, shrugging his shoulders. T.J. then sat up and both of us sat back, leaning against the fence. I thanked God for letting me escape another time. I thought for sure the Jeep Man had us this time.

"The Jeep Man's probably so mad!" I told T.J.

"He's probably driving all over looking for us," he said as he got up and crouched down on the ground preparing to look through the knothole.

"Or maybe he just got fed up and went home," I said as I got up and joined T.J.

"Hey, what's he doing?" T.J. asked as he stared out through the hole.

I looked through a crack and saw the Jeep Man's jeep parked at the end of Guajome. I then saw a boy standing beside the jeep. "I think he's talking to someone," I said.

"Can you see who it is?" T.J. asked.

"That's what I'm trying to figure out," I told him as I squinted through the crack trying to make out the figure. After peering a little bit longer, I told T.J., "I think its Chris." Chris lived on Catalejo a few houses down from T.J. I had no qualms about him, but Chris was one of a long list of kids who T.J. had picked on.

"Why's Chris talking to the Jeep Man?" T.J. asked.

"I don't know," I told him. But due to Chris' history with T.J., I feared it could not be good on our part. And as we continued to stare, the Jeep Man's jeep turned around and started to drive off.

"Good, maybe he's going home," T.J. said.

"I know. I..." I said, but before I could finish my words, we watched as the Jeep Man turned at an angle directly facing us.

"What's he doing?" T.J. asked as the Jeep Man came closer.

"I wonder if he knows where we are?" I asked.

"Nah, there's no way he saw us," T.J. said

But I did not share T.J.'s optimistic outlook, as I watched the Jeep Man drive up the dirt and park alongside of the fence we were hiding behind. "He knows," I said, as we quickly turned away from the fence and bolted in the opposite direction. We ran around the side of the house and up to the gate. I jiggled the door, but the latch that opened the gate was locked.

"Hurry, open it!" T.J. yelled.

"I can't. It's locked," I said as I shook the gate with extreme force. Time was ticking quickly. We could not afford to be tampering with this lock with the Jeep Man right behind us.

"Just screw it," T.J. said in frustration. I took my hands off the lock and started to climb over the gate. From the top, I jumped to the ground and waited for T.J. This side of the gate was much easier to climb due to the wood that could be used as handles, so T.J. would not have that much difficulty. T.J. soon appeared at the top of the fence and then jumped to the ground, landing much better this time.

"Let's get out of here," I said as we left the house and took off running down the street. Knowing the Jeep Man, he would be searching the backyard thoroughly, which would buy us a couple of minutes. But before long, the Jeep Man would soon be hot on our trail once again.

"Wait up, Ian!" T.J. yelled. I had always been faster that T.J., but with that cast on his arm T.J. must have felt like he was running with a ten pound weight.

"Come on, we're almost there," I said, hoping to motivate him. There would be plenty of time to rest once we reached our destination. I was heading for the main wall. Standing at about five feet tall, our main wall was pure white and encircled the entire ranch. For now, it'd make a great hiding spot if we could make it there without the Jeep Man spotting us.

"Come on, T.J. Just a little bit more," I told him as we left the sidewalk and ran into the open plain. This part of the ranch had no houses built upon it and had been cleared of tumbleweeds and bushes. It was perhaps the most dangerous area in the neighborhood. There was nothing to hide behind, and if one of our enemies spotted us we would make all too easy prey.

We sprinted on for about a minute with our lungs feeling like they could burst at any moment. But then, after what seemed like an eternity, we made it to the main wall. At five feet, we climbed it easily and then hopped to the other side. On the other side of the wall were hundreds of bushes that ran alongside the wall. The bushes had been planted there for decoration, but now T.J. and I used them for a hiding place. We crouched down between the little area that lay between the bushes and the wall.

With the Jeep Man probably still searching the backyard, T.J. and I sat hidden, preparing ourselves for a long wait. After narrowly escaping the Jeep Man a thought ran through my mind. It had plagued me throughout today's chase. I looked at T.J. and said, "I gotta go to the bathroom. Bad."

"Then go," T.J. said. Sometimes the greatest problems have the simplest solutions. I walked down a couple of feet and relieved myself, and then sat back with T.J.

"Feeling better?" he asked.

"Much," I said with satisfaction.

"How long you think he's gonna be out there?" T.J. asked.

"A while at least," I told him. "He's probably driving all over looking for us."

"I wonder how he found us back there," T.J. said, referring to the Jeep Man spotting us in the backyard.

"I guess Chris musta told him," I said.

"Man, when I get my hands on him!" T.J. said as his face angered with thoughts of the future punishment he would inflict on Chris. T.J. and I continued talking for about thirty minutes, when I peeked over the wall and said, "The jeep's back." It was the sign I had been waiting for. With the jeep parked in front of the trailer, we could be assured that the Jeep Man was safely inside.

We got out of the bushes and walked the long way home. As we headed back to Guajome, we spotted Chris down the street. "Hey, Chris!" T.J. yelled. Chris' eyes bulged like a street dealer who had just spotted a cop.

We ran over to him, cutting off his exit. I looked at him and said, "Why'd you tell the Jeep Man where we were?"

Chris was obviously terrified at what T.J. might do to him. His skin was pale and his body was shaking. He looked at me, knowing I was his only hope, and in a rattled voice said, "I didn't know that he was after you guys. I just told him where you were."

"What'd you think he was gonna do for us, buy us a Christmas present?" T.J. asked angrily.

I put my hand in front of T.J.'s body, giving him the signal to hold off for a second. Chris had been talking to the

Jeep Man for more than a few seconds. They had had an in-depth conversation. "What else did he say to you?" I asked.

Chris paused for a second and then saw T.J.'s fuming face. He looked at me and said, "He said T.J. broke into some of those model houses, and that he has a picture of it. He said he was gonna arrest T.J. at the bus stop Monday morning." I was blown away. T.J. had broken into one of the houses. No one owned the model houses. They were only to show prospective buyers, but nevertheless it was still breaking and entering.

"You can go now," I said to Chris as he thankfully scurried off.

Dumbfounded, I looked at T.J. with a puzzled look. Before I could say anything, T.J. said, "I didn't break into any houses."

"He said he had a picture," I told him.

"I don't know, but I didn't break into any house." he said. "I'm gonna go tell the Jeep Man right now that I didn't.

"Are you crazy?" I said.

"I gotta tell him I didn't do it," he said.

"Fine. You didn't do it, but going to the Jeep Man isn't the answer," I said. "He obviously wants to arrest you, and that's what's gonna happen if you talk to him."

"Then what do I do?" he asked.

"I don't know," I said, "But we'll figure something out." As I walked my friend home, I could not help being a tad suspicious. Had T.J. finally gone over the edge? Was this the moment we had all foreseen? T.J. had done a lot of horrible things and I could not help but wonder if this was just the next one on the list.

CHAPTER 8

The Fugitives

There was not much time. The sentence ran through my head like a never-ending loop. Father time cast his spell and laughed as I watched the world dance around me at an alarming rate. I scurried around my room, stacking up comic books and placing baseball cards in old shoe boxes. I threw my clothes in the hamper and stuffed my toys underneath my bed hoping they would be out of sight. The clock was ticking, and the minutes flashed by like lightning.

I had been issued the command, "Do not go anywhere until your room is clean!" But my dad was not aware of the crisis at hand. I had to get over to T.J.'s house, so we could settle matters with the Jeep Man. T.J.'s freedom depended on it. I shoved objects into the abyss known as my closet, knowing full well that my dad would just glance over my room. I glanced at the clock and shrugged at the amount of time that had gone by. I begged father time to be merciful but my cries fell on deaf ears, as my room still resembled a junkyard.

I decided to throw etiquette out the window. Whatever lay on the floor would be thrown into the closet. I threw clothes, school books and toys into the closet until my floor was clear of junk. I made my bed, then went downstairs, brought the vacuum cleaner up, and vacuumed my room. With the job completed, I smiled in triumph as father time's evil scheme had failed.

With my chores finished, I was now ready to start with my plan. A monumental event was about to occur. In our previous encounters with the Jeep Man we had been on the defensive. Now with T.J. in dire trouble, we were forced to play the offensive with the Jeep Man, whether it be creating a truce or an all-out attack.

First, I'd have to get the rest of the gang together. Jeep man was too tough and cunning for T.J. and me to handle alone. If it hadn't been for a generous amount of luck, T.J. and I would be sitting in the corner of a jail cell. I telephoned James, Harold and Dan. Due to parental incarceration, James was not allowed to go outside. Harold was not quite up to par with the Jeep Man yet, but I told him to stand by in case he was needed. I had told Dan to come over, but had not told him the reason why. There was not enough time to debate with him.

Within a few minutes, Dan was knocking at the door. "Hey, Dan," I said as I opened the door and walked outside.

"Hey, Ian," he said. "So where are we going today?"

"We're going over to T.J.'s," I said as we walked down my driveway.

"That's cool," he said. "I want to be San Francisco if we play," Dan said, referring to T.J.'s Nintendo football game.

"Well, actually were gonna do something else," I told him.

"What's that?" Dan asked.

Well, you'll never guess what happened yesterday," I said to him.

"What?" he asked.

"The Jeep Man," I said, answering his question.

"The Jeep Man," Dan said in a disheartened voice.

Eagerly awaiting to tell of yesterday's events, I said, "Yeah, T.J. and I barely got away from him yesterday."

"Oh, no," Dan said in a frightened tone. "What'd you guys do?"

I could see the terror in his face just at the mention of the Jeep Man. I tried to tell it to him gently as I said, "Oh, what we usually do. It was really fun." Along the walk to T.J.'s house I explained to Dan the whole story from the Jeep Man chasing us to T.J. being wanted. "So we gotta go back up to the Jeep Man and help T.J. get out of trouble."

Dan's skin turned paler than its usual ghastly color. He stopped walking and said, "Ian, if we go up there he could catch us. And we could get in trouble - not play-around trouble, but real trouble."

"I know, but if what Chris said is true then we really have to help T.J.," I told him.

Dan looked at me extremely panicked and asked, "So wait, T.J. broke into one of the houses?"

"No, that's just what the Jeep Man says," I said, hoping to convince Dan.

"Wait a minute. Just because T.J. said it doesn't mean it's not true. This is T.J., for gosh sake. He does bad stuff all the time," Dan said.

"Yeah, but if it isn't true then we gotta help him," I told him.

"Yeah, but if it is then we could end up going to jail with him," Dan said.

"Dan, don't worry. I'm not gonna let either of us get in trouble. Trust me," I told him. We continued the debate up until T.J.'s house. I did not tell Dan, but I was not completely sure of T.J.'s innocence. He was definitely capable of committing the crime. But perhaps it was just the thrill-seeker in me or perhaps I just wanted to find the truth. Either way, I wasn't going to miss out on this.

Once at his house, we knocked on the door. T.J.'s little brother Brendon answered the door. "Hey, Bren," I said to him.

"What do you want?" he said.

"What do you think?" Dan asked. "We want to see T.J."

"Well, you shoulda said that, you dumb head," he said as he walked away leaving the door open. We walked into the living room to find the other Sullivan brothers, Ryan, Corey and T.J. Ryan was the second oldest of the Sullivan brothers and the only brother to have dark brown hair. He was the most sensible one of the clan and often helped keep T.J. in line. Next to Ryan sat someone I had never seen before, and they were all staring at the television watching T.J. play Nintendo.

T.J. glanced over at us and said, "Hey, guys," as we took a seat upon the crowded couch. "This is my friend Jerrid." Dan and I both introduced ourselves to Jerrid and began to watch the television set with the rest.

After a few minutes of watching T.J. play, I looked over at him and said, "So, are you ready?" T.J. sure seemed unusually calm for a boy who could be living his last few hours as a free man.

"Yeah, but I'm not sure what I should do," he said.

"Well, I was thinking about it last night and I guess we could send him a note or something saying that you didn't do it," I told him.

"That's a good idea," Corey said. "I'll go get some paper," he said as he ran off into another room.

"You think it'll work?" Dan asked.

"Well, there's nothin' better to try," I told him. In a matter of seconds, Cory came back in with a pen and a sheet of paper and handed them to T.J.

T.J. looked up at me and said, "Okay, so what do I write?"

"Well, we'll start it off by saying 'Dear Jeep Man' and then in the middle we'll tell him that you didn't do it. And then we'll sign it 'The G.C. boys,'" I told him.

"What's 'G.C.' stand for?" Dan asked.

"That's just a name I call us. It stand for Guajome and Catelejo," I told him.

"But I don't live on Guajome anymore," Dan complained.

"It's just a name," I said.

T.J. began to jot down some stuff on the paper, but after a few seconds he crumpled it up and said, "This is taking too long. Let's just go down there."

I found it very peculiar for someone who had been accused of a crime to not want to use every resource to acquit himself. I stood up and said, "Well, okay. Let's hurry up and go, then." T.J. turned off the television and we all left the living room. We left the house, leaving Corey and Brendon behind. At six years old, Brendon was the youngest Sullivan brother and was too young to go off adventuring with us and too young to be left alone. So that left the next youngest Sullivan brother to watch him. Corey, the creator, did not mind though. Sometimes he would spend the whole day in the house just constructing masterpieces.

So off we went, leaving the two youngest Sullivan brothers and heading out towards the Jeep Man's territory. We had had a number of classic battles with the Jeep Man, but this time was different. As dangerous as it seemed at times, our skirmishes with the Jeep Man had no purpose other than escaping him. This time we all had a common goal. We all shared the same objective, to get T.J. acquitted. The Jeep Man would not rest until he had captured T.J. and sent him off to jail. We had to be extremely careful, for the fact that we were now trying to clear T.J.'s name made us accessories to the crime.

But as dangerous as this all was, I could not help but feel a little jealous. The Jeep Man's number one focus was T.J. I always assumed the final battle would be between the Jeep Man and myself. I reminded myself that for once, the adventure was not the most important objective. Clearing T.J. was our number one priority.

I continued thinking of the Jeep Man as we made our way to his territory. The six of us went down Catalejo, then down Guajome and finally over to the Jeep Man's area. We stood at a distance, with the safety of the school fence gone. I was not sure how we would get away from the Jeep Man this time. We had barely escaped him yesterday. Now with six of us there the odds were definitely in the Jeep Man's favor.

We stood out there, each of us looking at each other to make the first move. Finally, T.J. looked over at me and said, "What do you want to do?"

"I don't know. I guess we get him out here," I told T.J. and the group.

"All right, when do you want to do it?" T.J. asked.

"I guess now's a good time," I said.

T.J. cleared his throat and yelled, "Jeep man! Hey, Jeep Man!"

"Come on, Jeep Man!" I joined in. Then in the next couple of seconds the Jeep Man came out of his trailer, giving us that all too familiar scowl. We all stared at him with our hearts frozen.

We stood as motionless as rocks, when I looked over and saw the unthinkable. We had surely put ourselves on the guillotine. Ryan had purposely ripped the yellow 'Please do not cross' tape that closed off one of the streets. This tape had been put up on streets that had unfinished houses built on them to keep cars from driving onto the street. Ryan's hasty act had obviously sent the wrong message to the Jeep Man. It was as if we had slapped the Jeep Man in the face.

The gang looked at each other as Dan asked, "What have you done?"

But before he could answer, I yelled out, "Run for it!" With no school fence to hide behind, we did not have time to wait for the Jeep Man to make his move. We were going to need as much distance between ourselves and the Jeep Man as possible.

We sprinted away from the Jeep Man with myself in the lead, T.J., Dan and Jerrid following closely, and Ryan bringing up the rear. We headed in the same direction T.J. and I had gone yesterday. This time though, we knew not to turn towards our houses, where we had almost trapped ourselves before.

We ran towards the main wall. Due to its numerous outlets, the wall wasn't as safe as the school yard fence, but it would at least buy us a couple of seconds. And, unlike the construction area, the path we were now taking had no obstacles for the Jeep Man to dodge. It was a vast wasteland. The Jeep Man would have a clear path towards us. The construction workers had cleared the whole area, so when they decided to build houses upon the land there would be nothing in the way.

But though the surroundings looked grim, we sprinted on. Now we could hear the Jeep Man's engine start up. Even though I was remarkably afraid, I tried to keep myself composed so I could think of a way out of this. Dan, on the other hand, looked terrified and did not care who knew it.

"It's too far," I mumbled too myself. The wall was a good distance away and we had already run past the houses T.J. and I hid in yesterday. If we kept this up at this rate, the jeep would catch us for sure. I looked left and right, but there was nothing. The nearest object was a couple of houses, but those were a half a mile away. There would be no escape routes to bail us out this time. We were in the middle of nowhere. I felt as if we had been thrown into the tiger's pit.

A shout of, "He's almost here!" came from Ryan. I looked back to see that Ryan's observation was correct. The Jeep Man was almost upon us and we weren't even close to the main wall

"He's gonna get us!" Dan yelled.

"Just keep running!" I said as the jeep came even closer. We had about ten seconds of freedom left as I turned to see the jeep right behind us. Luckily, a thought popped into my head, and I yelled, "Split up!" T.J. and I glanced at each other, and then both of us took off in different directions. T.J. took off towards the right while I made my way towards the left.

"I'm coming with you!" Dan yelled as he ran alongside of me while Jerrid and Ryan ran off with T.J. Looking back, I could see that it was working. While both groups ran in different directions, the Jeep Man slowed down, bewildered by the group splitting in to two. The Jeep Man drove straight ahead, staying on his course, unsure of whom he should go after. This was a blessing from above because it was giving us the all too valuable time to reach the great wall. The Jeep Man was now forced to make a decision as we were almost upon the wall. And then he did, the Jeep Man veered right, making his way towards T.J., Ryan and Corey.

With the Jeep Man off our back, Dan and I ran up the hill that lay next to the wall and then hopped over it. We bulldozed through a couple of bushes. Then, once we were on the sidewalk, we sprinted toward T.J.'s house. We ran along the wall trying to make it to the entrance that led to all our houses. Hopefully, T.J. was holding his own. At this very moment, he was probably having the fight of his life with the Jeep Man.

Huffing and puffing, we made our way down the street. We were almost upon the entrance when Dan yelled out, "Oh, no! He's coming after us!"

I turned my head to see the Jeep Man had finished with T.J. and was now barreling down on us. He was a good distance away, but at 60 miles per hour, it would not take long to catch up. "Come on, Dan!" I yelled, motioning with my hand for Dan to catch up.

"He's gonna get us!" Dan yelled back.

"Just keep running!" I yelled as I turned into the entrance and ran down the street and headed towards T.J.'s house.

"He's gonna get me!" Dan yelled, still not at the entrance yet.

"Hurry, Dan! Hurry!" I yelled in the middle of the street.

I turned my head to see Dan turning into the entrance and yelling, "He's right behind me!" Dan was exaggerating a little bit but the Jeep Man was close.

I finished crossing the street and sprinted up T.J.'s driveway. I ran up to his door, opened it quickly, and yelled, "Come on, Dan. You're almost there!"

Dan crossed the street, continuously yelling, "He's gonna get me! He's gonna get me!" Dan had to hurry and make it into the house before the Jeep Man spotted him. Otherwise, all of us would become bunkmates at the local prison.

"We are so dead," I thought to myself as I waved Dan in. Brendon and Cory stood behind me waiting to see what all the commotion was, but I did not have any words to spare. The Jeep Man knowing where one of us lived would be like Lex Luthor uncovering the secret identity of Superman.

"You're almost there!" I yelled as Dan ran through the doorway and dived into the carpet. I slammed the door shut, ran to the window, and watched as the Jeep Man drove by.

"What happened?" Dan asked, not yet having picked himself up off the floor.

"We did it!" I yelled, jumping up in triumph.

"Great," Dan mumbled with his head planted into the carpet. I laid back on the carpet next to Dan and began giggling to myself.

"What happened?" Cory asked.

"The Jeep Man was chasing us and he almost got us," Dan told him as he still lay on the ground.

"Yah, we were all running, and the Jeep Man was..." I stopped momentarily as my eyes widened.

Dan looked at me and said, "T.J." I went back to the window and gazed outside. I looked up and down Catelejo and what I saw scared me. There were kids playing and sprinklers spraying, but there was no sign of T.J. or the rest. The Jeep Man must have caught T.J. He was probably handcuffed in the back of a squad car getting ready to spend the next ten years behind bars.

If there were a chance of saving him, it would have to be now. Not much time had passed and there might still be enough time left to make a difference. I looked to Dan and said, "Dan, we gotta go get T.J."

"Are you crazy?" he asked. "We just barely got away from him."

"Come on. It'll be fun," I told him.

"Yeah, that was a barrel of laughs," Dan said sarcastically.

"We have to go. We can't just leave him out there," I said.

"All right, all right. I'll go," Dan said unenthusiastically. "But you'll have to give me a couple of minutes. I'm too tired right now."

There was not enough time though. By the time Dan caught his breath T.J. would be on his way to jail. "I guess you can stay here," I told Dan. "But if I'm not back in a while, I'm gonna need you to come and get me."

"Sure," Dan said with a slight grin on his face. He was obviously ecstatic that he was being left behind.

"Ok, see ya later," I said as I opened the door and left the house. I crouched down and tried to stay beneath the plants, making sure to keep an eye out for the Jeep Man. He could be anywhere. I would have to go back to the trailer to see if he was holding T.J. and the others hostage.

I crossed Catelejo and slithered through the grass of the vacant lot across the street. Once I reached the main wall, I stood up, climbed it and dropped to the other side, landing safely behind a wall of bushes. I poked my head out of the bushes, not sure what I would see.

As my head emerged from the shrubbery, my eyes widened in astonishment. T.J., Ryan and Jerrid were walking down the street towards me. I jumped out of the bushes, startling them, and said, "Hey, you guys!"

"Hey," T.J. said, a bit surprised.

"I thought the Jeep Man had gotten you guys," I said.

"We thought he had got you," T.J. said.

"Where's Dan?" asked Ryan.

"He's back at you guys' house," I said. "We barely got away from him. I came back to get you guys."

"We barely got away from him too," Ryan said. We traded war stories as we headed back to the house. T.J. opened the door and we all walked in. Dan walked around the corner munching on a few chips he had taken from the kitchen. "You found them?" he asked.

"Well, yah, but the Jeep Man didn't get 'em," I said.

"Nah, we got away," T.J. said. We all went into the living room as T.J. relayed their escape to Dan.

After all the stories were done, Dan stood up and said, "I'd better get home for dinner." We all got up to walk Dan out. T.J. opened the door and we all gasped in horror as the Jeep Man drove by. Running on instinct, T.J. quickly slammed the door.

"What was he doing out there?" asked Jerrid.

"He must know where we live," T.J. said.

"Probably not. If the Jeep Man knew where we were he'd be knocking down this door right now," I said. "He's probably just going through the neighborhood looking for us."

"What are we gonna do now?" Dan asked.

"Wait," I said as we went back into the living room. We sat around, some of us playing video games while others played

Monopoly. We ate, drank, and plotted our next counterattack against the Jeep Man.

Before we knew it, a couple of hours had passed and Dan looked up and said, "I really gotta get home."

"I guess it's a good enough time to try it again," I said. We all proceeded to the door again. This time we opened the door ever so slowly, making sure there would be no surprises. Then Dan and I slowly crept out the door.

"See ya guys later," Dan whispered as if the Jeep Man was around the corner.

"Bye, you guys," T.J. said, and with a wave, we left T.J.'s house and headed down Catelejo.

"So, why do you think the Jeep Man was there?" Dan asked.

"I'm not sure. But when he was chasing us, he might have figured out what streets we live on," I told him.

"Aw, no," Dan said. Dan's worries were justified. If the Jeep Man knew what streets we lived on, he was that much closer to finding out where our houses were. As I pondered this topic, we left Catelejo and started walking down Guajome. While walking down the street, we passed James' two younger sisters jumping rope in the middle of the street.

"Hey, you guys," I said as I passed them.

Leah, the older of the two, ran over to us and said, "I talked to that security guard." Our eyes bulged, as we knew she was referring to the Jeep Man.

"What'd he say?" Dan asked.

"He asked where you guys were," she said. I became extremely alarmed. It was dire consequences for all of us. The Jeep Man had always used a defensive strategy, but if he were to start continually patrolling the streets, it would only be a matter of time before he had us.

"And what'd you say?" Dan asked.

"I told him I didn't know, cause I didn't know where you guys were," she said. I breathed a sigh of relief. You could always count on Leah to be trustworthy. A major catastrophe had been avoided.

"Good job, Leah," I said, congratulating her on her effort.

"But," she said with a wicked grin on her face. "I told your Dad."

"Told him what?" I asked.

"How you guys are bothering that security man," she said.

"Why'd you do that?" I asked exasperated.

"Because you boys are bad and should not be bothering the man," she said. Obviously the cunning Jeep Man had had his way with this simple life form. I should have known. There was only one creature more conniving, more wicked, and more untrustworthy that the female species, and that was the young female.

Walking away in frustration, Dan and I left the two harpies and headed across the street to my house. "What are you going to do?" Dan asked.

"Guess I'll head home and see how much trouble I'm in," I told him. Problems like these were always best when confronted immediately. Then you could have the rest of the day to have fun with no regrets. We walked up my driveway and then over to my doorway. "You wait here so I can be yelled at," I said. "Be back in a minute."

I opened the door expecting a barrage of lectures. I looked around and saw nothing. Then I could hear the footsteps from upstairs. There was nothing I could do. I bravely stepped in front of the firing squad with my eyes bandaged and a cigarette in my mouth. Sure enough, my dad walked downstairs with a look that told me that the rifles were cocked and loaded. "Were you bothering that security guard?" he asked.

"No," I said. I had to remember it was my word versus the word of a nine-year-old girl.

"That's not what the girl across the street told me," he said. I headed back to the door. "Where do you think you're going?" my Dad asked.

"I have to take Dan back home," I said as I grabbed the doorknob.

"I'd better not hear of you and that security guard again," he said. "And don't be hanging around that T.J. Dave already said he was one of the main suspects in some break-ins." I ignored my dad's words as I headed back outside.

"So how'd it go?" Dan asked.

"Aw, you know," I said, not really wanting to talk about it. "I'm not sure how we're going to get you home. The Jeep Man's probably going through the neighborhoods right now looking for us."

"But I have to go home pretty soon and eat dinner," Dan said.

Thinking for a couple of seconds, I headed down the driveway and said, "Come on."

"Where we going?" Dan asked.

"We're going back and getting the rest of the guys," I said. With the Jeep Man patrolling the neighborhood for us, there was only one safe route in which to take Dan home. We would have to go around the neighborhood instead of through it. So we headed back up to Guajome and over to Catelejo and up to T.J.'s house. After knocking on the door, T.J. opened it and said, "Back already, guys? I thought Dan had to go home."

"I was gonna take him, but I saw Leah and she said the Jeep Man's driving around looking for us," I told him. Jerrid and the rest of the Sullivan brothers gathered around to hear the conversation. "So, I'm gonna need your help in getting Dan home."

"Then let's do it," T.J. said as he waved Jerrid and Ryan on.

As we left the house, I said, "I figure we'll have to take the long way around, so we won't bump into the Jeep Man." We left his house once again and walked towards the main wall. It covered the entire neighborhood and would take us all the way to Dan's new house, which lay on the other side of the Jeep Man's territory.

After a few minutes of walking alongside the main wall, an idea leaped into my head. "Hey, if the Jeep Man's looking for us, then he's not at his house, right?" I asked the group.

"So?" T.J. asked.

"If we go through his house, then it should be pretty safe," I said.

"I don't know," T.J. said.

"Well, that's the way I'm gonna go," I said.

"We'll keep going this way and meet you," T.J. said.

"I'm coming with you," Dan told me. So with a wave good-bye from Dan, we split into two groups once again. Dan and I walked downward toward the construction site while the others continued on along the wall. Dan looked over to me and said, "Do you think he did it?"

"Who did what?" I asked.

"Do you think he broke into those houses?" Dan asked.

"I'm not sure," I said. "I guess if he says he didn't we gotta believe him." I was not exactly confident of my own words. Deep down, I knew there was a good chance T.J. had at least been involved with the break-ins. With the rumors of T.J.'s drinking and drug abuse that ran rampant in the neighborhood, I was not sure what to believe.

Suddenly, we heard the sound of an engine nearby. Dan got a panicked look on his face and started to look for a place to hide. Listening for a little bit longer, I said, "Don't worry. It's not the Jeep Man." Reluctantly, Dan stood by as we waited and watched a Cadillac drive by. I had been in enough incidents with the Jeep Man that I could easily pick out the sound of his engine.

Dan, still agitated, looked at me and said, "Maybe now'd be a good time to meet the others."

"Yah, I guess so," I said as we cut towards the main wall. We walked away from the Jeep Man's territory and over towards the spot at the main wall where I calculated their whereabouts to be.

After a few minutes, Dan and I had reached the wall and Dan asked, "Do you see them?"

"Nope, but keep looking," I said to Dan. "They're around here somewhere."

"Sure hope we see them and not the Jeep Man," Dan said.

"Me too," I told him.

"There they are," Dan said pointing them out.

"Hey, guys!" I yelled as we crossed the street to join them.

"We think we saw the Jeep Man," said Corey.

"We'd better hurry up and get him home," I said. We walked along on the opposite side of the street from the main wall. We walked down the street, past the dried-up canal and over to the stoplight. I stopped for a second and glanced up at the mountain. I gave it a quick smile and then caught up with the rest of the gang. We crossed the street and were now walking alongside the lake.

At this time of the day, the setting looked spectacular. A crimson sunset was in the sky and seemed to give the lake a reddish hue. I stared at the lake and admired its beauty. Perhaps tomorrow would be a good day to go fishing. We could wake up early, find some worms and head out to the lake while the fish were still out.

My thoughts of tomorrow's events were broken up when T.J. yelled, "Jeep man!" I looked back and saw the Jeep Man speeding down the street; we left the sidewalk and took off running towards the lake. We bulldozed through grass that reached up to our thighs, hindering our escape.

Since I had been lost in thought, the others had a considerable lead on me. They all hid behind a big pile of brush that lay near the iron gate around the lake. The Jeep Man was coming and I did not have enough time to make it to the hiding spot.

"Hurry, Ian," I heard Dan yell. With the brush too far ahead and the Jeep Man coming down the street, I jumped into a patch of tumbleweeds. We then all sat quietly as we held our breaths and watched the Jeep Man drive by and out of sight. With this, the Jeep Man had missed his last chance for the day. We finally had a safe passageway to take Dan home.

Our hectic weekend with the Jeep Man was finally over. It had definitely changed our relationship with the Jeep Man. T.J. was wanted. We were his accomplices, and the Jeep Man had some idea of what neighborhood we lived in.

The fun and games we played with the Jeep Man were now over. And T.J. would somehow have to escape him at his bus stop. I was not worried though. T.J. would find some way out of it. He was as resourceful as they come. With the stakes so high with the Jeep Man, I could not help but wonder if we all were up to the task. I knew the Jeep Man would be.

CHAPTER 9

ID Mountain

It was another sweltering summer day in the city of Moreno Valley. With temperatures soaring into one hundreds, I lay on my bed and wondered why I was cursed with a father whose values seemed to come from the middle ages. Why was I made to be put through such inhumane cruelty? No human, or animal for that matter, should have to endure such horrible torture. Why could my dad not just flip a switch, give us relief and let the air conditioner do its job?

Due to a severe case of extreme thriftiness, my dad would not turn on the air conditioning except in extreme cases. I guess his son dying of a heat stroke did not qualify. So upstairs I lay in my bed, sweating like an exhausted marathon runner, trying to forget the summer heat. My room was layered in its usual filth of comic books and baseball cards scattered across the floor. I read the latest issue of Silver Surfer, and as I turned the pages I let the metallic superhero whisk me away from the torturous temperatures to cosmic battles that held the fate of the galaxy in its outcome.

I read with extreme concentration, hoping that the surfer could come through just one more time, for our planet depended on it. But the fate of the universe was put on hold when my mom yelled out, "Ian, get the phone." I put the comic book back in its plastic case, threw it on the floor and ran downstairs to the kitchen. My mom handed me the phone and said, "It's Dan."

Picking the phone up, I said, "Hey, Dan. What's up?"
"Hey, guess what?" Dan asked anxiously.
"What?" I asked.
"I've got some really great news," he said, sounding even more anxious.

"What is it?" I asked, thinking Dan got a new pack of basketball cards.

"My parents are going to be going away for a couple of days and they want me to stay at your house till they come back," Dan said rather quickly.

The news was good, but not in the least earth-shattering. "Oh, that's cool," I said in a rather mundane voice.

"No, you don't get it," Dan said, apparently not finished with his announcement

"Well, what?" I asked now with my curiosity piqued.

"This is our chance," he said. "We can finally go up to the mountain and spend the night."

"What did you say?" I asked Dan, wanting him to reaffirm his statement.

"Now we can finally go up and spend the night at the mountain," he said. Now, this was front page news. I had always dreamed of the night where I could leave society behind and spend the night at the mountain. Thanks to Dan, my barbaric dream would become reality.

"Good thinking, Dan," I said.

"Yah, well, you know," Dan said in a boastful manner. But he had every right to be cocky. Usually I had to drag Dan kicking and screaming to get him to partake in an adventure.

"Wow, I gotta admit I'm surprised," I told him. "You usually hate to do this stuff."

"I know, but this is going to be fun," Dan said. This seemed somewhat peculiar. Where was the cowardly, craven boy I had grown up with? Had some demon from another dimension possessed my best friend, leaving me with a new, exciting Dan?

Not wanting to ruin the moment with any negative statements, I said, "Man, we're gonna have the best time." The wheels in my brain had already began to spin as I told him, "We'll have to go in my garage and get my tent and we'll bring food and we'll make a big list so we don't forget anything. This is going to be so cool."

"I know, I can't wait," Dan said eagerly.

"Here, I'll come over and then we can plan and stuff," I said.

"All right, I'll see you in a little bit," Dan said.

"See ya," I said, as I hung up the phone. I quickly put on a pair of shoes and sprinted over to Dan's house. Once there, we went straight to his room, where we mapped out our plan with military precision. We repeatedly went over detail after detail until the plan was flawless. And it would have to be impeccable, for the wrath of our parents hung in the balance.

So I devised an ingenious plan where Dan would tell his parents that he was spending the night at my house while I would tell my parents I was spending the night at his. Then tomorrow we would camp out at the mountain and return home before Dan's parents did. Napoleon himself could not have constructed a more elaborate scheme.

After putting the finishing touches on the plan, I headed home. Once there, I fed my dogs, took off my clothes and went to bed a tad bit earlier than usual. I had hoped by going to bed and falling asleep earlier that that would also bring the morning sun up earlier.

It seemed to take an eternity for the sandman to make his nightly rounds. But finally my eyes shut, and when I opened them it was glorious morning. I threw off my covers and searched through the pile of dirty clothes that engulfed my room. After selecting a T-shirt and some shorts, I quickly dressed myself and then gargled a slab of toothpaste so my mom would not noticed that I hadn't brushed my teeth. I went downstairs and quickly devoured the breakfast my mom had made me. Then I put on some shoes and headed down to Dan's house. After a five- minute walk through the Jeep Man's territory and through the school, I arrived. Dan's sister let me in, and I walked upstairs to Dan's room to see him on the ground playing football on his Sega video game system.

"Hey, Dan," I said as I sat down beside him.

"Hey, Ian," he said while still playing the game. "Man, I can't wait."

"I know. Me too," I told him. "Guess what?"

"What?" he asked.

"I thought of a super good idea," I told him.

"What is it?" he asked curiously.

"Well, we can go get Vincent's raft and take it up to the mountain. Then at night time we can go out on the lake and go swimming and stuff," I told him.

"Hey, that is a good idea!" he said as we shut off the game and television.

"Let's hurry up and go over to my house so we can get started," I told him, not wanting to waste any time.

"Oh, my parents are already gone, but I almost forgot to tell you, my mom gave me this note to give to your mom," Dan said. Dan's mom was the sweetest woman on the planet and it didn't take Sherlock Holmes to figure out what the letter said. I opened it up and read it quickly. It told of how grateful Dan's parents were for letting him stay over our house. As sweet and sincere as it was, it was tragic that this note would never reach its final destination.

"I think we'll just keep this in here," I said, as I crumpled the note and stuffed it into my pocket. We both then proceeded downstairs and outside where we made our way over to my house once again. Once there, I got the key to my garage and opened up the door. There have been dumpsites cleaner than our garage. There was discarded junk all over the place. There were boxes filled with my father's old school books, unused tools and all sorts of cleaning products that had not been used.

"Hope the tent's still good," I told him. "We haven't used it in a while." The last time it had been used was when we first went up to the mountain. I had not cleaned it out then and hadn't bothered to since.

"Hey, there it is," Dan said, pointing to the top shelf. It was behind a couple of old boxes that held my old Star Wars toys. I reached up to the top shelf, grabbed it and threw down the duffel bag, which contained the tent.

"All right, well, now the tent's taken care of," I told him.

"So what else do we need?" Dan asked.

Looking around the garage, I told Dan, "I think that's it from the garage. Now we gotta go get the sleeping bags and I gotta get some clothes."

"We're gonna need some food, too," Dan said.

"Yeah, we'll get that at your house." I didn't want my parents wondering why all the lunch meat had suddenly disappeared. Before shutting the garage door, I took out the note and tossed it into a sea of garbage never to be found. "We can just leave that here."

So Dan and I went inside, where we searched the house on our scavenger hunt. Luckily, my parents had gone to the store and we had free access to the house. Once we were finished raiding the house, we stood out on my driveway with the equipment laid out in front of us. At our feet lay two sleeping bags, a pillow case and a couple of sticks of beef jerky I had been saving for a special occasion.

After getting all the supplies from my house, we went down the street to borrow the raft. We walked three houses down to Vincent's house. His family was Indian, and he didn't come outside too much. But he was a nice kid who could be trusted. We often traded comic books and talked neighborhood talk.

Then after talking to Vincent and promising not a single scratch would come to his raft, he reluctantly gave it to us. We brought it down to my house and set it down with the rest of the supplies. The raft was amazing. It looked like a real raft, not one of those cheap kiddy ones you found in Toys R Us. It was yellow with blue stripes and seemed large enough to fit three or four people when inflated. Unfortunately, Vincent had not been able to find both oars and we were stuck with only one.

We began to check our inventory, making sure we had not forgotten anything. In the midst of our inspection, two of the neighborhood girls, Anna and Katie, showed up behind us. These girls roamed the neighborhood as much as we did. They didn't do much though; they just nosed around like curious new reporters waiting for a solid lead. I never understood how the girls in the neighborhood could just be content with jumping rope and playing dress-up. Didn't they know there was a world of adventure all around them? Dan turned to them and said, "What do you guys want?"

"We're just seeing what you guys are up to," Anna said as her eyes surveyed the supplies in front of us.

"Nothing," Dan said, a bit peeved by their appearance.

I looked over at Anna and said, "Well, we're..."

"Aw, Ian, don't tell them," Dan said, cutting me off.

"Tell us what?" Katie asked as she stood awfully close to Dan.

"None of your business," Dan answered as he took a step away from Katie. Katie had had a crush on Dan for about two years, and Dan claimed that he hated Katie's guts. But because Katie saved both of us in one of our adventures, we succumbed to her wishes and agreed that on Dan's fourteenth birthday they would go out on a date. Even though his fourteenth birthday was many years away, Dan would still plead to be let free of his bargain.

"They won't tell," I said, trying to reassure him.

"They're girls, Ian. They'll tell," he said. It was a valid point he had brought up. Girls were loathsome, treacherous and could not be trusted. But out of the whole evil lot, there were a minute few that could be trusted. These girls were like sisters to me, and I counted them among the few who held my faith.

"Don't worry, Dan," I said

"Aw, man," Dan said in disappointment.

Turning to the girls, I said, "Dan and I are going to go up to the mountain and spend the night up there."

"Your parents are going to let you?" Anna asked.

"Of course not, dummy," Dan said. "We're not going to tell them."

"Whoa, and what's that raft for?" Katie asked.

"We're gonna take it up to the lake," I said.

"That's neat, you guys," Anna answered. "And you guys are taking all this stuff up there?"

"Yep," I answered.

"Aren't you guys going to be scared?" Anna asked.

"No," Dan said snapping at Anna. "We got a lot of stuff to do to get ready, so we'll see you guys later." Finally getting Dan's subtle message the girls took off down the street. "Man, I thought they'd never leave. You have gotta let me out of that deal."

"Hey, a deal's a deal," I told him. "Let's hurry up and get this stuff over your house." We packed up all the small items in my duffel bags and carried the rest of the larger items in our hands. We then walked down Guajome carrying two bags filled with the tent and my clothes, a pillowcase that contained some beef jerky, a raft with an oar, and two sleeping bags. With all this equipment, a turtle could have beaten us back to Dan's house.

Eventually, after an extremely long journey, we made it to Dan's house. We laid our provisions down in his garage and went inside the house. When we opened the door, Dan's older sister walked by, catching a glimpse of our equipment. "What are you guys doing with all that stuff?" she asked.

Dan and I looked at each other cautiously. Telling Anna and Katie was due to the bond I shared with the girls. Telling Rachael was just an act of stupidity. She stood for everything that girlhood represented. She was untrustworthy, corrupt and truly evil incarnate.

Looking at Rachael, we both said, "Nothing."

"Yah, right," she said sarcastically.

"Really, we're not doing anything," Dan said to his sister.

The evil beast looked at Dan and said, "I know you guys are up to something, and if you don't tell me then I'll tell Mom."

"But Rachael," Dan pleaded.

"I mean it. I will," she said coldly.

Dan looked at me hoping I had some solution. I just shrugged my shoulders and gave him the approval to tell his sister. Dan looked back at his sister and said, "We're gonna go spend the night up at the mountain."

"Gross! Why would you guys want to go spend the night up there?" she asked.

"We just do," he said.

"You boys are dumb, "she said. "But don't worry, your secret's safe with me." And being appeased, the wicked demon banished herself to her room.

Dan and I then went into the kitchen, where we opened one of the cabinets and grabbed a plastic bag for our food. We opened up the fridge as we prepared to invade the kitchen. We grabbed some slices of cheese and two sodas, then placed them in the bag. We then went to another cabinet, took out a loaf of bread and a bag of Dorritos and placed them in the bag with the rest of the food.

Once finished, I went out to the garage and placed the bag of food with the rest of our supplies. Meanwhile, Dan was upstairs packing some clothes for himself. Once he was done, he came downstairs and laid his bag with the rest of the equipment. We stared at all the equipment with a look of despair. "Would you look at all of that?" Dan said.

"I know," I agreed. Before us lay two sleeping bags, an oar, a raft, two bags filled with clothes, two pillows, a tent and a bag full of food. We had barely managed to make it to Dan's house, and now we had even more supplies to take all the way up a mountain.

"We're never going to make it up with all this," Dan said.

"I know," I told him. "We're gonna need some help."

"Aw, Ian. Not him," Dan said, already knowing who I was thinking of.

"Hey, we need help and he's the closest," I said, speaking of Harold. He lived on the other side of Dan's house and was always willing to lend a hand. Dan found his lies very bothersome, but for the moment, he was the right boy for the situation.

"But Ian," Dan protested.

"And we gotta get this stuff up here before it gets dark or else we'll be in tons of trouble." I told him.

"Aw, man," Dan whined.

"Just call him," I said. Dan walked off to make the phone call and I began pulling the equipment into the driveway.

A few minutes later, Dan came back and said, "All right, I called him."

"Good, now help me get the rest of the stuff out," I said, referring to the equipment that was still in the garage.

We had begun pulling the rest of our supplies onto the driveway when Harold rode up on his bike. "Hey, Harold," I said as I pulled the raft onto the driveway.

"Hey guys," he said as he got off his bike.
"Hi, Harold," Dan said in an unappreciative voice.
"What's up?" I asked Harold.
"I was going to go over to Angela's house and hang out with her on the couch, but I guess I'll just help you guys out," Harold said. Angela was the prettiest girl in the neighborhood. She wouldn't give Harold a second glance, and she would never invite him inside her house.
"Yah, right," Dan whispered to me in a sarcastic tone. "In his dreams."
"Are you guys almost done?" Harold asked.
"Yah," I said as Dan pulled the last item onto the driveway.
"Ok, is that everything?" Dan asked.
"That should be it," I told him. "All right, let's do this." I picked up the duffel bag and pulled it over my shoulder, put the bag containing my clothes on the other shoulder and carried my sleeping bag with my right hand. Dan had the bag that held his clothes, his sleeping bag, and the bag with the food. Harold took the raft and our pillows and carried them on his bike. So off the three of us went, each carrying a tower of supplies that could topple at any time.

As we walked down the street toward the mountain, the sun had begun to set and the scorching heat had begun to fade. We walked past the school and then past the lake, having to stop five times to pick up fallen equipment. By the time we hit the mountain, the sun was about to leave while the temperature had reached absolute perfection. The hike up the hill was extremely difficult and if we had to have hiked a few more yards we might not have made it. Once we had reached the top of the hill next to the split boulder, we flung the equipment to the ground and fell on top of it.

"Boy, am I glad that's over," Dan said.

"Me too," I said as I rubbed my left shoulder, which was a little sore from carrying the tent.

"I sure wish I could stay with you guys," Harold said for the two hundredth time. The whole way there, Harold had bombarded us with subtle hints of him wanting to camp out with us.

"I know," I told him. "But you're still new. Once you've done more stuff with us, then you can come to the big stuff." This was the first time we were camping out at the mountain and there was no way I was going to let an unaccomplished rookie join us. Harold spending the night at the mountain would be like a man stumbling upon a bottle of vintage wine and drinking it as if it were a common beer.

"Are you sure?" Harold asked. "Cause I've camped all over the country."

Dan and I rolled our eyes. I looked at Harold and said, "Don't worry, by the next time we go, you'll be able to come. But we better hurry up and get this tent up 'fore it gets dark." With a few minutes of daylight left, the three of us rushed to put the tent up. We unhitched the poles, slid them through the sockets, and then redid the process after figuring out we had put the poles in the wrong slits. So, after going through the process again, by the time we finally erected the tent, the moon was up. I looked at the others and said, "Good thing we finished. If we'd taken any longer it'd be too dark."

"Is that it?" Harold asked.

"Yah, the tent's all taken care of," I told him.

"I better get home then, 'fore my mom gets mad," he said.

"Ok, we'll see ya later," Dan said.

"Yah. See ya later," I said. "When you go, take that path over there," I said, pointing to a road that was the quickest and safest way out.

"If I stop by Angela's house, I'll say 'hi,'" he said as he hopped on his bike and rode down the path.

"Oh, God," Dan said. "He never stops."

"Who cares now?" I asked. "Let's try this tent out." We picked up our sleeping bags and threw them in the tent. We jumped on our sleeping bags and stretched out. We lay on our backs and stared at the ceiling.

After a few seconds of admiring the structure, Dan asked, "So what do we do now?"

I thought for a second and said, "I guess we can blow up the raft." Dan ran outside and brought in the raft. I rolled over onto my stomach while Dan laid out the raft. Luckily, there were two air holes on opposite sides for both of us to use.

Dan and I began blowing with all our might into the air holes. We took large breaths and blew it all into the raft. Each of us huffing and puffing, we took a break for a few minutes and then continued blowing. After one of Dan's tremendous exhales, he looked at me and said, "Ian."

"Yeah," I answered, using the moment to take a breath.

"I wish it was always like this," he said.

"Like what?" I asked.

"I wish it was summer and never school," he said.

"Me too. I wish it could always be summer," I said as we continued blowing up the raft. The raft slowly rose, as we exhausted our bodies. As the minutes rolled by, I noticed that the raft seemed to move. I watched as it moved farther away. Then my eyes started to lose their focus as the tent began to swirl.

I then heard a sluggish voice from Dan mutter, "Ian." I looked over to see Dan lying down on his back hardly moving. I tried to move next to him to see what was wrong, but my body suddenly collapsed to the ground. When I looked down, the ground was spinning. I clutched my sleeping bag, trying not to be whisked away. The tent started to fade to black. I closed my eyes and breathed in deeply. I forced myself to remain calm. I tried to concentrate on happy thoughts as I reminisced about Silver Surfer's latest exploits. After rehashing the surfer's most recent adventure, the dizziness finally began to fade from my mind. I opened my eyes to see that the world had stopped spinning. I crawled over to Dan and said, "You o.k.?"

"Yeah," he said. "I almost passed out."

"I know. I think I almost did too," I said as I rolled back onto my sleeping bag, still feeling a slight queasy. We lay there for minutes, until Dan finally sat up and said, "I'm starting to feel better now."

I joined him in sitting up and said, "Me too."

"What happened?" he said.

"I guess we were blowing too fast. This time when we blow it up, we'll go real slow," I said. We looked at the raft to see it standing about three-quarters full. This time, we took our time blowing it up. After each moderate puff, we took a rest for about ten seconds and then started again.

And then finally, Dan said, "That should do it." We plugged up the air holes and looked at the raft.

"I guess we'd better take it down there before it gets too late," I said. I grabbed the raft while Dan grabbed the oar and the flashlight and brought them out of the tent. We left the tent site and made our way down the main path. With one hand each of us held a side of the raft. I held the oar while Dan led the way with the flashlight. Once off the path, we made our way around the gorge, where we could now see the lake.

Dan shone the light at the lake and said, "I don't think I'm going to go swimming in that."

"Why not?" I asked.

"It's gross," he said.

"But that's what makes it more exciting," I told him.

"Ugh, no way," Dan said disgustedly.

"Your loss," I said as we walked down the hill towards the lake. This was the side of the lake that no one was allowed on. This was the side past the danger buoys. But it had deteriorated much more since T.J., Dan and I took the paddleboat on it. The ranch owners had abandoned this side of the lake and let it rot into a putrid swamp. The water was murky brown, with lily pads lying throughout. Most of the lake had been covered by a thin layer of plants growing on top of the water while other parts had huge stems piercing the surface of the lake. It was revolting. It was gross. It was not fit for human consumption. It begged to be swum in.

We walked down to the edge of the swamp as Dan said, "I'm definitely not getting in that."

"You're gonna be missing out." I took off my shirt and shoes and then laid them down on the ground. Dan put the flashlight by my shoes and we laid the raft on the water.

"Here goes nothing!" I yelled as I jumped into the water.

It was always better to get used to the water all at once than to tortuously drag it out. Once in, I felt a bit uneasy. There was sludge everywhere. It felt as if I were swimming in a pool of jelly. After quickly resurfacing, I looked over to Dan and said, "Get in." Dan laid the oar into the raft and then got in it. I gave the raft a push and let it float out into the lake. Dan pulled out the oar and began paddling as I swam alongside.

"How's it feel?" Dan asked about the water.

"It's not that bad," I said. "You should try it."

"No thanks," Dan said with a look of disgust on his face.

"Too bad," I said as I dunked my head under the water, but even I was not brave enough to open my eyes in the toxic waste. I resurfaced and wiped the water and a leaf from my face.

We continued out further into the marsh when Dan said, "Look at that!" Dan shone the light in the middle of the lake. I looked over and saw a small creature resembling a rabbit entangled in some of the plants. Its body bobbed up and down while its arms wiggled frantically trying to free itself. His efforts were to no avail, as the sludge seemed to overtake him and bring him under for a final time.

If my heart had not suddenly been stopped by fear, I might have had a chance to swim over to it and try to save it. Now all I could think about was getting back in the raft. Dan was obviously thinking the same thought when he suggested, "Maybe you should get in the boat."

"Yah, maybe," I said, agreeing with him as I tried unsuccessfully to erase the creature from my mind. Dan scooted to the back of the raft bracing it for my arrival. I grabbed onto the raft and pulled myself into it. The water seemed to slither off me.

Once completely in I asked Dan, "You ready to go back?"

Dan flashed the light behind us making sure we had a safe route and then said, "I'm ready to go." I took the oar and began paddling back to the shore. Within a few minutes, we were there. We got out of the boat and pulled it onto the shore. I grabbed my shirt and shoes and put them on. I grabbed the oar and then both of us took hold of the raft and started to head back to our campsite. As we walked towards the hill, Dan said, "Boy, am I hungry."

"Me too. Those sandwiches are gonna taste so good," I said.

"And I...augh!" Dan screamed. "A spider!" In trying to fling the spider away from his body Dan sent the flashlight to the ground. It made a loud noise as it collided with a rock beneath us.

"What happened?" I asked.

"A spider got on me," he said, still checking his shirt to make sure nothing was on him. I bent down to pick up the flashlight, which was not shining anymore. I picked it up and flipped the switch on and off a couple of time. It gave no reaction. "Is it working?"

"Nope," I said as I handed the useless equipment over to Dan.

"You can hardly see anything without the light," Dan said. He was right. The mountain looked like one huge dark shadow.

"Let's just hurry up and get back," I said which would be a bit harder with no light guiding the way. We made our way back, tripping over cracks, walking in prickly tumbleweeds and slipping into a few holes. Eventually, we reached the top of the hill. It had taken us at least twenty more minutes going up than it did on the way down.

We laid the raft and oar down, as Dan said, "I can't wait to eat." We walked into the tent and Dan quickly pulled out the bag of food while I took out a change of clothes. I put on some dry clothes while Dan scoured through the bag. Once fully dressed, Dan handed me four slices of bread, two slices of cheese, a handful of tortilla chips and a couple of sticks of jerky.

"Where's the meat?" I asked.

"There isn't any," he said, taking a second look.

"Are you sure?" I asked. Dan waved an empty bag to satisfy my curiosity. We went through all the bags making sure we had not stuffed the ham into any of our clothes. Perhaps the meat had fallen into a pocket. But after looking, we had no such luck.

"Dang it," Dan said.

"We'll just eat em' like this," I said as I took a bite out of my sandwich. We quickly scarfed down the food. Neither of us even noticed the missing meat. It was a feast worthy of kings.

Once the banquet was over Dan and I crawled into our sleeping bags. "Man, that was good," he said as he patted his belly. "I never knew cheese sandwiches could be so good."

"Me, neither. And that jerky hit the spot," I said. We chatted on, praising the taste of the meal. As the conversation went on for the next ten minutes, I watched as Dan's eyes bobbed up and down.

"See ya in the morning," I said, as I had grown tired of watching him struggle to keep his eyes open.

"Good night, Ian," he said as he shut his eyes for a final time. I lay in bed for a bit, but it was not long before I fell asleep to the rhythm of the crickets chirping.

Then suddenly I awoke. But it was not morning yet, for it was much too dark. My throat was extremely dry, but Dan and I had drunk the last of the sodas. I looked over at Dan sleeping quietly. His mouth was open and he was probably dreaming of making the winning shot in the NBA finals. I crawled out of my sleeping bag and slowly and silently unzipped the tent and went outside. Quickly a rush of cool air ran against me.

I walked over to the split rock and climbed on top of it. I gazed out into the city. At this time of night, there was not much activity. Normally, I could see hundreds of cars driving about. I was not sure how late it was - I would guess somewhere between two and three in the morning. As I gazed upon the city, I thought back about what Dan had said earlier. He spoke of how he wished things could remain the same.

I wished they could too. I wished we never had to get older. I wished we never had to die. There had to be some way you could live forever. There had to be. I wished I could stop time and remain a kid forever. Today's events would soon be yesterday's memories. Even as I sat upon this rock, time marched on, but I would never let time change me. I would be a kid forever. I would never become some mindless adult zombie, who could only follow the idiotic ramblings of the masses. I could beat death. I knew I could.

Our adventures had given me a feeling of immortality. I felt unbeatable. If anyone could beat it, I knew I could. I had to. I looked up into the heavens for an answer. I received none. With my eyes starting to drag, I decided to go back to sleep. Whatever the secret of death was, it would have to wait to be solved on another night. I crawled off the rock and walked back to the tent. I tiptoed back into the tent, zipped it up and crawled into my sleeping bag. I closed my eyes and thought of future adventures as the sandman took me away.

I awoke the next morning to the sounds of Dan rustling in his sleeping bag. I opened my eyes to see Dan getting out of his bag. "Did ya sleep good?" he asked.

"Ok." I said. "I sure am thirsty." My throat was still extremely dry. All I could think of was some form of liquid running down my parched throat.

"Are there any sodas left?" Dan asked.

"No, I checked last night," I told him.

"I could have sworn we had more," he said.

"Maybe we dropped one on the way up," I said. "Let's go look." I got out of the sleeping bag and put my shoes on. Dan and I went outside, where we were flooded with extreme brightness. We stretched out our arms and adjusted our eyes to the light.

"You take this side and I'll take the other. Then we'll meet back here," I told him. Dan walked off in one direction while I walked off in the other. I searched around rocks, cacti, and tumbleweeds. It was all to no avail. After having walked quite a distance away, I began to make my way toward the campsite. If there was nothing to drink, we would have to hurry home. As I went back, I saw something that resembled a water fountain. Were my weary eyes deceiving me? I ran closer and saw that it was indeed a water fountain. "Dan, Dan!" I yelled. "Come here!"

Eventually, Dan's head appeared from a distance and asked, "What is it?"

"Water," I yelled back. Dan ran down the hill towards me so excited he tripped over a rock, almost landing on a nearby cactus.

Once Dan had reached me he said, "Wow!" I had been so excited, I had forgotten to take a drink. I turned the fountain on and drank the water. It was the sweetest-tasting water I had ever had. We went back and forth slurping the water until we were both full.

As I wiped the water dribbling down my mouth, I said, "I wonder why this fountain's here?" This was the first time I had ever seen it.

"Who cares?" Dan asked, taking another sip. Although the fountain had been our savior, it seemed strangely out of place. I worried it could be the work of future developers. Our city, once completely rural, had been overtaken by mad constructors who were building everywhere. I decided to worry about it another day as we headed back toward the tent.

With a long day behind us, we packed up the supplies, pulled down the tent and made our way home. It would take an extremely long time since we did not have Harold aiding us. However, this time we placed all the supplies in the raft and dragged the boat home. And after a long walk, we arrived at Dan's house, where I did not stay long. I decided to go home quickly so my parents would not be suspicious.

A couple of hours later as I sat in the kitchen, the phone rang. I picked up the phone to hear Dan say, "Ian, you're not gonna believe it."

"What?" I asked.

"Rachael told my parents," he said.

"She what?" I asked, hoping I had heard wrong.

"She told them that we spent the night at the mountain," he said. I looked over at my Dad on the couch reading the newspaper. He would be furious if he knew that I had spent the night at the mountain.

"Don't worry though," Dan said. "It took a while but I talked my parents into not telling your parents."

"You did?" I said as I breathed a sigh of relief.

"I'm going to be grounded for two weeks," he said, "but it was worth it." Dan's quick thinking deserved a reward. I thought for a few seconds and said, "You know what, you don't have to go on that date with Katie."

"I don't?" he said. "Thank you, thank you, thank you." Dan and I talked for a little while longer; then I got off the phone and went over to his house. Once there, we both apologized to his parents and promised it would never happen again. I began helping him with the chores he had received as punishment. While we worked in the backyard, we picked up weeds and talked of the fantastic night we had had.

"You know what?" I asked him as I pulled a weed out of the ground.

"What?" he asked.

"I can't wait till we get to do it again," I told him with a grin on my face.

He looked at me as he put another weed in the trash bag, and said, "Me too."

CHAPTER 10

The Sewers

It was a terrifying time for kids in the neighborhood, for all around us were signs of the apocalypse. Water bills soared as the number of daily scrubbings rose. Gas prices quadrupled as cars made frequent trips to clothing stores where mothers torturously made their children try on thousand of clothes for their morbid amusement. Our hair was chopped off and primped, so that we would be somewhat presentable to our future masters. All this meant only one thing: school was on the horizon.

Kids played throughout the streets getting their last few days of summer in before the cursed 'first day' came upon us. It was a time of artificial joy and prolonged sorrow. It seemed forever since the final bell had rung on the last day of school and we had run through the school yard leaping in enthusiasm. We had all known in the back of our minds that our freedom was nothing but a three-month long parole.

So, on one of my last days of freedom, I walked to the recreation center sulking, yet still trying to savor the last few morsels of my summer days. I walked up to the iron gate that surrounded the lake and the recreation center. I surveyed the area intensely. As I looked from left to right, a family van pulled up and I watched as a father brought his two daughters for a swim in the pool. I waited as they entered the pool hall and left my range of sight. With the family gone, the area seemed safe and secure. I quickly climbed over the iron gate, landed on the ground and then took another look. Luckily there was no one around, but more importantly the Dragon Lady was nowhere to be seen. I had been taught on a numerous occasions that just because the Dragon was out of sight did not mean she was not nearby.

In fact, I was almost positive that she was. For since it was a blistering summer day, the pool was sure to packed with kids, and the hierarchy of the ranch would be sure to have their strictest enforcer there keeping everyone in line.

I crouched down and walked alongside the gate toward the lake, trying to blend in with the scenery and stay out of sight. I walked along the gate until I reached the shrubs that signaled the end of the iron gate. I had walked past the pool hall, but I still was too close to the Dragon Lady. I walked down to the tip of the water and then began to walk along the lake out of sight of the Dragon Lady. The walk seemed to last forever, but I didn't mind. I cherished each second. I wished these last few days of summer could go on forever no matter how wearisome they might be. I would easily take a boring day of summer over a tedious day of school. After a while, I came up to the tunnel near the danger buoys. I looked back at the recreation center. I was definitely out of range and would only look like an indistinguishable speck to the Dragon.

Standing at the edge of the lake, I gazed out into the water. The lake was at peace; it stood motionless with the occasional ripple from an unfortunate insect that had misjudged its height and landed into the water.

I took my shirt off and threw it a good distance away from the water. I breathed a sigh of relief as a breeze ran about me, soothing my body. I then took off my shoes and socks and laid them down next to me. I sat down along the edge of the water and placed my feet in the lake. I did not know what heaven was like, but it could not have felt better than the sensation my feet were experiencing in the cool water.

I stretched my arms out as the feeling of extreme comfort began to make me feel a tad drowsy. Seeing a nearby rock wedged in the dirt, I pulled it out and threw it out into the lake. I watched as the rock hit the water and set out ripples throughout the lake and up to my legs. As I continued to watch the ripples die out, I realized that today was going to be an extremely dull day. This was fine by me though, for we had had enough heart-pounding excitement for one week.

My mind began to wander and I thought back to that fateful night. Dan and I were outside around nine o'clock having one of our usual debates.

"But Ian, I could get in trouble," Dan said with a worried face.

"You won't get in trouble," I said, trying to reassure him. "No one will even know what we are doing."

Still not reassured, he said, "Isn't this illegal or something?"

"It's not illegal," I said, not knowing fully if it was illegal or not.

"B...b...but," he stammered.

"Trust me," I said as I crouched down with a screwdriver in my right hand. "It'll be O.K. Just come on and help me."

"I don't know," Dan said.

"Just come on before someone does come in and catch us," I said accidentally.

But it was already too late, for in my hurry to get the job done I had blurted out the wrong words. Dan was a fragile kid who needed constant reassurance. One tiny slip would cause his self-esteem to shatter. "I think I'm just going to go to the pool," he said, having made up his mind.

"Man, Dan," I said, annoyed, ashamed and disappointed all at once.

But before I could continue our debate and convince him to stay, he hopped onto his bike and said, "I'll see you tomorrow." I breathed a sigh of disgust as I watched the yellow-skinned chicken ride off on his bike.

Sometimes I just did not understand Dan. We had to have lived in one of the most exciting neighborhoods in the world, yet he would rather go for a swim than partake in a great adventure. Didn't he see all that I was doing for him? I was taking him away from the mindless zombies of our society and bringing him into a life of excitement and intrigue. I guess some people just weren't appreciative. But with time fading quickly, I took my mind off Dan and put it to the mission at hand.

Due to the T.J. incident, matters with the Jeep Man were escalating like an uncontrollable fire. We were going to need a more permanent place of safety. At the rate this crisis was growing, even our houses weren't safe. The Jeep Man knew what neighborhood we lived in and it might not be that long before he tracked us down to one of our houses.

So I had begun thinking of a location where we could escape the Jeep Man on a moment's notice. Days of thinking went by as I tried to find the perfect place. The mountain was too far, for on a good day, it took twenty minutes just to reach its base, and by that time we'd be playing the harmonica in some prison cell. The unfinished houses were a good idea, but the Jeep Man patrolled them too much and the Dragon Lady policed the lake with an intensity that matched the Jeep Man's. As frustration grew, I began to give up on the idea until an inspiration finally came to me.

It happened as I stood outside after just washing my driveway down with the hose. I took a small stick and placed it into the water that ran down the gutter. As it flowed down the gutter floating down the street I ran alongside to keep up with it. Then I stopped as I watched the water flow down the street and into the drain. It struck me instantaneously. The sewers would be the perfect hideout. I was furious with myself for not thinking of it sooner. It was too perfect. The sewers were out of sight, they were close, and they could even lead us to a safer part of the neighborhood while the Jeep Man searched frantically for us. I immediately began preparing for how we could use the sewers to our advantage. It didn't take long for me to come up with a scheme, and not wanting to wait, I figured tonight would be the perfect time to implement my plan.

Now, ready to execute the plan I had concocted, I gazed at the pothole that lay beneath me. It was somewhat rusted with sand covering a lot of it. At a diameter of around two and a half feet and made of solid metal, I had my work cut out for me. It had to have weighed at least sixty pounds.

With my screwdriver in hand, I dug around the edge of the pothole, expelling as much of the hardened dirt as possible. The dirt did not come up easily, but with a little force it finally started to give. The pothole obviously hadn't been removed in years. It felt as if it hadn't been removed in decades. But I enjoyed it nevertheless. I felt as though I were some famous archeologist unearthing a treasure that had been lost for centuries.

I continued digging, scraping along the edge of the pothole and brushing the dirt aside every couple of seconds. Occasionally, a car would drive by and I would quickly place the screwdriver behind me and wait for the car to pass by. Except for the occasional curious glare, I experienced no trouble and went on with my work with no hindrances. After a few minutes of digging, I brushed away my final pile of dirt and laid my screwdriver down on the sidewalk. Still crouching, I blew around the edge of the pothole, getting out some of the dust I had missed. There was still some dirt, but I hoped I had made enough impact to get the pothole off.

Picking up the screwdriver once again, I rammed it up against the pothole, making sure to wedge it tightly. The end of the screwdriver now rested underneath the cover. I pushed down on the handle hoping to pop the sewer lid off. I pushed as hard as I could, wishing now that I had superhuman strength. My muscles strained and I felt as if the screwdriver would bend under the pressure. I let go of the screwdriver as the strain had become too much. I shook my hands and blew on them, hoping to relieve the throbbing pain. But after a few seconds, I tried again and found myself once more with my hands throbbing from the pain. This job was too tough. I was going to need help. With Dan AWOL, I would have to get one of the others. And since I happened to be in Dan's neighborhood, I figured Harold would be the boy for the job.

I walked down the street, keeping the screwdriver in my pocket, for a boy walking down the street in the middle of the night with a screwdriver in his hand would arouse too much suspicion. I walked down the street, and then walked onto Harold's. Luckily I caught him outside riding his bike. I ran up to him and said, "Hey, Harold."

"Hey, Ian," he said, returning my greeting. "What are you doin' over here so late?"

"I was getting ready to come over to your house," I informed him. "I need some help."

"With what?" Harold asked as he circled around me on his bicycle.

"I'm trying to get into the sewers, but I need your help to get in there. So can you help me?" I asked him.

"Yah, I can help," he said.

"Thanks," I said, appreciative of Harold's willingness.

"So what do we need to do?" he asked.

"First I'm gonna need something more than just this screwdriver," I said as I pulled it out of my pocket to show him. "So I figure we'll go over James' house and get the stuff we need."

"Are we going right now?" he asked.

"Yah," I answered. "We should go before it gets too late. And you'd better leave your bike here cause we don't want to leave it out while we're in the sewers."

"All right," he said as we walked up to his house and put his bike in his garage. Then, after a five-minute walk through the neighborhood, we arrived at James' house and knocked on his front door. James' youngest sister, Suzanne, opened the door and then led us into the house.

"He's in his room," she said as she ran into her room upstairs. We walked into James' room, where we found him lying on his bed looking over some of his old football cards.

"Hey, guys," James said as he put down his cards.

"Hey, James," Harold responded.

Not having much time to spare, I said, "We need your help."

"With what?" he asked.

"Harold and I are going to go explore the sewers and we wanted to see if we could borrow some of your stuff to take over there. You can come too, if you want," I told him.

"My dad won't let me out this late, but I can help you get the stuff you need," he said.

"Well, that's cool," I told him.

"So what do you need?" he asked.

"Come on into the garage and I'll show you," I told him. The three of us walked into James' garage and started to look around. James' dad had the best tool set of anyone in the neighborhood. There was a plethora of tools at our disposal.

After looking around a bit, James walked over to me and said, "So, you decide what you want yet?"

"First, we're gonna need some light," I told him.

"I'm not sure where the flashlight is," James said. "I think one of my sisters was messing with it."

After looking around at the inventory a little bit more I said, "That's o.k. We'll just make torches and use that for light. That way, we'll be more like real explorers."

"Cool," Harold said, delighted at the idea.

"What d'you need for that?" James asked.

"We'll use these sticks over here," I said as I picked up two pieces of wood. "Then we'll need some cloth, to burn on the end of the sticks. And then you'll have to get us some hair spray and a lighter."

"All right, I'll go get everything," James said.

"And while you're gone, I'm gonna go get my backpack to put everything in," I said as I ran across the street to my house. I ran upstairs, picked up my lucky backpack and left the house. Luckily, my parents were watching a movie on television and had not even noticed that I was in the house. I returned to James' garage to find Harold watching James cut up one of his T-shirts.

Once James was finished, I gathered the items he had gotten for me, put them into my backpack, and said, "You ready to go, Harold?"

"Yah, this is gonna be cool," he said.

James looking a tad disheartened since he would not be able to explore with us and said, "I'll at least walk you guys down there."

"That's cool. Then you can help me get the sewer cover off," I said as we opened up the garage door and made our way down Guajome.

"This is going to be so cool," Harold said.

"I know. I can't wait," I said.

"You guys sure are lucky," James said, obviously wishing he could join us.

Then a thought quickly sprang into Harold's head as he said, "Are we gonna stop off and pick up Dan?"

"No. That chicken was supposed to be helping me earlier, but he got all scared and took off," I said.

"Well, that's Dan for ya," James said, knowing Dan all too well. The three of us continued to walk down the street, walking past the Jeep man's territory, through the school and over to the pothole.

"Well, we're here," I said.

"So, you guys are really gonna do this?" James asked.

"Heck yah," Harold told him. "This is gonna be so fun."

"All right, let's hurry up and get started," I said as I took off my backpack.

I unzipped it and pulled out the screwdriver. James looked at it and asked, "What are you using that for?"

"To try and open this thing," I told him as I pointed the screwdriver at the pothole cover.

"And you couldn't open it last time?" Harold asked.

"No, but now James is here," I told Harold. I hated to admit it, but James' strength had surpassed mine. His chubby exterior had transformed into a muscular one. In fact, his strength had surpassed any kid in the neighborhood. This was an amazing feat since he was a couple of years younger than I was. We all figured that someday he would be a football player for the Oakland Raiders.

"Let's hurry up, before my dad notices I'm out this late," James said.

"Ok, give me a hand here," I said as I wedged the screwdriver underneath the cover once again. James and I both pushed down on the screwdriver until we started to see some results.

"Hey, it's moving," Harold said. As James and I continued to strain our muscles, the cover slowly crept up. We grunted as the top finally popped up completely.

"We did it," James said as we both let go of the screwdriver and rested.

But not wanting to wait any longer, I nudged James on the shoulder and said, "Come on, let's get it all the way off." We both got up on our knees and began pushing the metal cover. It was enormously heavy and moved very slowly. But within a few seconds, the cover was completely off.

I poked my head down the hole. There was nothing to be seen but total darkness. But an intense odor of rotten eggs was so overwhelming it made me stick my head out. "Man, it stinks in there," I said.

"Did you see anything?" Harold asked.

"Nah, it was too dark in there," I answered. "I guess we better light the torches up." I kneeled down to the backpack and pulled out the sticks, cloth and the hair spray.

I handed the hair spray to James and one of the wooden sticks to Harold as he asked, "Now what do we do?"

"Put the parts of the T-shirt around the end," I told him. We both began wrapping the cloth around the end of our wooden sticks until we had used up the cloth.

"Can I do it now?" James asked anxiously.

"Yep, start it up," I told him. James sprayed the cloth on the end of our sticks making sure to wet down every part.

Harold watched in amazement as he said, "This is gonna be so cool!"

"All right, light us up now," I told James. He flicked his cigarette lighter and brought forth a tiny flame. He then brought the flame over until it was touching my cloth. The cloth instantly caught flame. With a glare on my face, I stared at it in awe.

"Do mine, do mine!" Harold said enthusiastically. James then lit Harold's and both of us stood there with two lit torches.

Holding the torch gave me a rush of raw power. I felt like Indiana Jones about to explore a pyramid that had not been opened for centuries. Now I eagerly wanted to get down into the sewer. I turned to James and said, "You better get goin' before you get in trouble."

"All right," he said in a bleak tone. "I'll see you guys tomorrow."

James walked off and I looked at Harold and asked, "You ready?"

"Yah," he said in an excited voice.

I handed him my torch and stuck the upper half of my body into the hole. I moved my arms around until I came across a ladder, which lay up against the wall. I came out and then reentered the hole feet first this time. I climbed down the ladder where I emerged into a room that was covered in spider webs. "Hand me the torch!" I said as I panicked.

He lowered down the torch, and I grabbed it, making sure not to burn myself. Once the torch had entered, the place immediately lit up. I was in some subterranean room that looked as big as my bedroom except the walls and ceiling were made out of cement. There were empty candy bar wrappers, soda cans and other forms of trash scattered about the room.

There were also spiders crawling all over, but not just any common arachnid. They were the most deadly, creepiest creatures of all, black widows. Their skin was as black as night, with a red blood spot on its fat abdomen. Their bodies were round like a bubble about to burst, and from their stomachs came tiny legs which resembled eight prickly needles. The black widow was the one animal which I truly feared. Each movement of the widow would bring me to a panic. With only one bite, it could send me to Lady Death. "Hurry up and get down here," I said, holding both torches so Harold could walk down.

Once he climbed down the ladder, I handed him his torch and we surveyed the area. The whole place reeked of rotten garbage. The stench was almost overwhelming, but the sight seemed to nullify the smell. This subterranean sewer resembled a medieval torture chamber.

"Wow!" Harold said in amazement.

"Yah, this is pretty neat," I said. We walked through the small room as I made sure to stay away from anything that resembled a black widow. Spider webs slithered over us as we made our way across the chamber. Once we reached the center of the room, I spotted something and said, "Hey, this is what I was looking for." I pointed to a small tunnel that reached up to my knees. It must have led outside the room. We both peered down into it, as it seemed to either run over to the other side of the street or perhaps down to the lower parts of the sewer. Every schoolboy knew that underneath the city lay sewer-like mazes filled with alligators, lizards and other hideous reptiles.

The tunnel had fewer spider webs than the room, which was perfect, since we would have to get in the tunnel to examine it. "Ok, Harold. Since you're smaller, you go first," I told him, still trying to hide my fear of the widows. Harold, eager to go, crawled into the tunnel with his torch, and I soon followed. We crawled like toddlers as we made our way down, exploring the tunnel. It was a tight squeeze, but we were able to proceed.

Surprisingly, the tunnel was a tad bit cleaner than the room we had come from. The cleanliness was probably due to the water that ran through it during the rainy season. As I pondered the tunnel's cleanliness, I spotted a tiny black figure next to Harold. As Harold crawled by it, it got startled and ran away from him towards me. As the dark blot crawled into my light, I quickly identified it as a black widow. "Ok, Harold. I think we've gone far enough for now," I said as the creature crawled towards me.

"All right," Harold said as he started his way towards the tunnel's entrance. The problem that this created was that as Harold moved backwards, the frightened spider would run towards me. I crawled back as fast as I could. Its legs moved rapidly as it came bearing down on me. Cramped in the tiny space, there was no maneuvering room. The spider would surely seize me and send its fangs into my flesh. I crawled back as fast as I could, but to no avail, as the widow was gaining.

Soon it was only two inches away from my right arm. This was the closest I had been to a black widow since I woke up with one on my bed when I was four years old.

With no brilliant ideas coming into my mind, I began to blow and spit on the spider. Luckily, confused or afraid, it started to move the other way. This was the break I needed. I continued backwards almost to the exit.

With Harold moving backwards, the spider turned around and started making its way towards me again. The spider had quickly regained its lost ground and was almost upon me once again. I would have tried to burn it with my torch, but I did not want to accidentally burn Harold. With the spider just centimeters from my face, I crawled out of the tunnel, falling on my rear and almost dropping my torch. The spider soon followed and ran up the wall towards the corner into the shadows. Harold then followed as he crawled out of the tunnel.

We both stood up and shook the cobwebs off ourselves. "So what'd you think?" Harold asked.

"It'll work," I said as I walked over to the ladder, still feeling a bit rattled. We climbed out of the sewer, pushed the lid back on, and took the remaining webs off our faces.

"That was cool," Harold said.

"Yah," I said. We placed our torches on the ground and stomped on them until the flames were out.

Harold looked down at his watch. It read eleven thirty three. He looked at me and said, "I better get home before my mom gets mad. I'll see you tomorrow,"

"See ya tomorrow," I told him. We took off in opposite directions and made our ways home. Although, I had been forced to confront a childhood trauma, I had found what I was looking for. We now had the perfect hideout from the Jeep Man. Sanctuary was now but a few feet away. I just had to determine which was scarier, the black widow's bite or the Jeep Man's wrath.

CHAPTER 11

Villains

Throughout history, with skirmishes ravaging throughout the earth, there have been men who, for whatever reason, decided to take a stand. There were men who took their destiny into their own hands. They fashioned themselves as immovable obstacles in the path of the forces of evil. Whether accomplishing or failing, these men bore the name 'hero.'

Some heroes' feats were momentous while others were faintly remembered. Some men saved entire cities while others simply pulled a cat out of the tree. Some had their heroic deeds passed down from generation to generation while others were only kept alive by the heart of a loyal child.

Many people seem to overlook the one person that made these men stand out. The one who tested these heroic men to their limits with his dire deeds was the dastardly villain. Villains were as vital a part in the legendary stories as the heroes themselves. Whether it be a cruel dictator or a deranged madman, the villain brought out the best in the hero. For these villains gave our heroes the passions and the means to accomplish their goals and fulfill their destiny. And as fate would have it, the greater villain saw his feats matched by an equally great hero.

While some villains were people, some heroes' antagonists were bizarre circumstances, while some were faulty ideas. But whatever form they took, the villains' goals were all the same. Their mission in life was to thwart our hero from achieving his objective. But one thing was certain, the hero would be nothing without the villain. For what would David be without Goliath, Robin Hood without the Sheriff of Nottingham, or Batman without the Joker?

Yes, villains play as much a part in our society as do our heroes and the same could be said for our neighborhood. Out of all our archenemies, the Dragon Lady, Max, Crazyman, et al., there was one man who stood above the evil pile, one man whose vileness hung over the neighborhood like a dark cloud. The Jeep Man was the cruelest, meanest, most sinister man we had ever met. He was the slayer of children, the crusher of hopes, and the defiler of dreams. He had long since replaced the boogieman as the number one terror in the hearts of kids in our neighborhood. Many kids just relinquished the right of safe passageway to the school. Many times I had come home to see the Jeep Man with a crowd of captured kids probably being sent off to some childhood prison.

Although I loved the adventures with the Jeep Man, of late they seemed to become different. The adventures had always seemed like a game, a dance with destiny. But of late, the mood seemed to change. The game was becoming grimmer. A scent of danger now seemed to loom around the neighborhood.

But on one serene day, I found myself at the park next to the school. I had taken my dog there to run and play in the outdoors. I would take my dog there many times and watch in delight as my dog would sniff scents, bulldoze through bushes or just lie about in the grass. We had no grass in our backyard and my dog loved the chance to wallow in its grassy stems.

I sat in the field, exhausted from running around chasing Lucy - trying to put the leash on her. She looked almost as tired as I was as she lay panting beside me. I laid back and let the sun shower my body. If only every day could be this wonderful. I had no school. I had no homework. I had no chores. Life could not get any better. As I lay back, almost falling asleep, I saw my dog swerve its head quickly. I turned to see the Jeep Man coming this way with his dog. He was coming after me and I was trapped. Lucy, being an overweight dog, would not be able to outrun the Jeep Man. And I could not leave my dog in the clutches of our worst enemy.

I decided I would have to stand and take my punishment. It seems the Jeep Man would finally get his justice. The Jeep Man walked up to the two of us. I cleared my throat and prepared for the inevitable. The Jeep man looked at my dog and then at me and said, "That's a nice dog you've got there."

Stunned and in shock, I managed to mutter, "Th – thanks." His dog then began running around my dog, jumping around it quite playfully. It seemed as if the Jeep man's dog had developed a crush on my Lucy, or perhaps his dog was just lonely. The Jeep Man's second dog had mysteriously disappeared from the neighborhood. I had just figured that the beast was not living up to its duty and the Jeep Man had relieved him of his command. Either way, it was quite strange to see the Jeep Man's dog act so playfully. The only memories I had of that dog were mean and vicious ones.

Luckily, it also seemed that the Jeep man didn't recognize me. He had never actually seen me face to face, and our neighborhood was layered with tons of kids. I had never seen the Jeep Man this close either. His face resembled the face of any normal man around his age. He had a few wrinkles in his skin and I could see a few specks of gray in his hair.

"So how long have you had her?" the Jeep Man asked.

"I've had her for a while - since I was about eight," I said, still feeling a bit awkward.

"She's still got a bit of pup in her," the Jeep Man said as we watched his dog chase Lucy around the park. "She's a good dog."

"Yah, she is," I said.

"Is she trained?" the Jeep Man asked.

"Not really, I kind of just let her do what she wants and she knows when I want her to do something," I said, still bewildered by the situation.

"That's the way you gotta do it," the Jeep Man said. "Some people believe you gotta forcefully train your dog, but if you give them a lot of love, sometimes that works better."

"Yah," I said, astonished at what I was hearing. After letting Lucy run around for a few more seconds, I turned to him and said, "Well, I'd better get her home." I did not want to take any chances. T.J. was still a fugitive and I did not want to wait for the Jeep Man to suddenly remember me.

"I'll see you later," he said as I walked off to get Lucy. I walked up to my dog, put the leash around her neck, and then headed home. I was dumbfounded at the whole situation. Had I misjudged the Jeep Man? Was he capable of kindness? He actually had seemed like a pleasant man. I pondered these questions on the way home and then for the next couple of days.

Then one night the struggle for control of the neighborhood became worse. It had been about a week since my meeting with the Jeep man and I had not heard any news concerning T.J.'s run from justice. I had not even seen T.J. lately and wondered what mischief he had gotten himself into. It was one of our last summer nights, as I lay on my bed sweltering in the heat. I decided to go outside and soak myself with the hose. Nothing would take the summer heat away quicker than a good drenching from the hose. I went downstairs and out the front door. The temperature outside was not much cooler than the temperature inside. Our nights were hotter than some of the days of other cities.

As I walked outside, I saw my next door neighbor Jennifer standing across the street. I walked past the hose, postponing my wet relief, and crossed the street to have a summer chat with Jen. During the summer nights in our neighborhood, many of the kids would hang out and converse since it was the only time of the day you could come outside without facing unbearable temperatures.

Having crossed the street, I walked up to her and said, "Hey Jen."

"Hey," she responded seeming a little unfocused.

"What are you up to?" I asked.

"I'm just waiting to see T.J.," she replied.

"Oh, no wonder," I said. It was common knowledge in the neighborhood that Jen had a huge crush on T.J. "Hoping for a little evening romance?"

"No, Ian," she said as if she did not know what I was implying. "I'm waiting to find out what else happened."

"Find out about what?" I asked.

"Didn't you hear what happened?" she asked.

"Uh, uh," I said.

"You mean you didn't know? How could you not know?" Jen asked.

"What? Tell me," I said now extremely curious.

"You mean you didn't hear about T.J. and that security guard you guys are always getting into trouble with?" she said.

"No, what?" I asked, now extremely curious. Jennifer took a deep breath and started to tell the story.

It seemed T.J., his friend Ken, and the other Sullivan brothers were playing in the construction area. Ken, who lived on the other side of the neighborhood, was the new kid in town. He looked a couple of years older than T.J. or me, and he looked like he was a member of a biker gang. He had long brown hair that he usually tied up in a ponytail. He was a little bit taller than I was, sort of fat, and his face was covered with acne and long, brown scraggly facial hair as if he were attempting to grow a beard. Most of us did not hang around Ken too much, but T.J. did, since they went to school and rode the bus together. They also seemed to share a similar lifestyle. Both seemed to have that uncontrollable, rebellious attitude.

Ken had an aura of trouble about him. Some rumors even suggested that he had spent some time in prison. Even scarier than that was his girlfriend. She actually claimed to be a real witch. There was talk that she dabbled in black magic and cast spells upon anyone who crossed her. I did not believe in that nonsense, but I kept my distance just in case.

Just hearing that Ken and T.J. were both in the Jeep Man's construction area alerted me to trouble. We took our chances when crossing the Jeep Man's territory, but it was suicidal to sit there and play in it. But that was just what they were doing. T.J. and Ryan were playing swords with some pieces of wood left over from the construction. The others sat and cheered at the fight.

Wooden sword fights were one of our favorite games and would be played whenever two sticks could be found. T.J. was an excellent swordsman. Many kids would surrender to T.J., not being too sure how far he would take the game. You could never tell when T.J. might lose his temper and ferociously start attacking you.

As they fought in the construction yard, Ryan hurled his sword at T.J.'s neck, but with a lift of his left arm T.J. easily blocked his attack. He then raised his arm in the air and, with a quick monstrous thrust, he struck his brother's sword out of his hand. T.J. motioned as if he were going to deliver the final blow and Ryan put his hand in front of his face preparing himself for it. Seeing this, T.J. raised his sword in the air, and proclaimed, "Yes, I beat you."

At T.J. strutted due to his victory, the others walked back slowly. After T.J. had stopped his chants of victory, he noticed six pair of widened eyes and three opened mouths. Perplexed, T.J. turned around to see what the others were so taken by. He turned to see a monstrous creature covered in darkness heading towards him. As it came into the light, T.J. recognized it as the Jeep Man's number one crony, his dog.

Apparently, the beast had been awakened by T.J.'s victory cry or perhaps it had detected the scent of one of its most chased prey. The Jeep Man's dog would sleep for hours underneath the Jeep Man's wagon. It usually was chained up, waiting to be called for active duty, but it was now free, and not too happy about having been woken up.

    The dog crept closer, starting to make its way towards T.J. It bared its teeth as it let out a low growl. T.J. walked back slowly as the others watched in disbelief. The dog began to throw out barks as T.J. still walked back slowly, trying not to make any sudden movements. The dog began barking rapidly as he started to jog towards T.J. T.J. trembled as he raised his sword in the air. With the dog now in range, T.J. took his wooden sword and swung at the dog. The blow came within inches of the dog's nose. The dog snapped at T.J., but T.J. kept him at bay by keeping the sword in front of himself and the dog. T.J. moved with the dog, making sure to keep the sword in between both of them.

    The dog barked fiercely as it seemed to be waiting for an opening. T.J.'s frightened eyes never left the beast. He knew that if he made one slip he would surely be torn to shreds. T.J. was trapped. If he ran, the dog would surely attack him, and staying here was only delaying the inevitable. But just when T.J. thought the situation could not get worse, it did. The door of the Jeep Man's trailer swung open and in the doorway stood the Jeep Man. It would seem that the barking had woken up the Jeep Man as he stood there glaring angrily at T.J. The beast still stood barking as if he were keeping T.J. cornered until his master could take him.

    T.J. swung at the beast, knowing full well that he had nowhere to go. The dog remained unfazed as it stood there holding T.J. hostage. He swung at the dog again and looked at the Jeep Man, trying to show him that he was not bluffing. "Keep your dog away from me," T.J. yelled frantically. The Jeep Man stood in the doorway for a few seconds, then he came out and took a few steps towards T.J., glaring at him intensely.

"I mean it! I swear I'll hit this dumb dog," T.J. yelled out desperately.

The Jeep Man stood there motionless, as if he were pondering his options. He then looked up and said, "And if you do that, I'll kill you." Then, to show that he was not playing around, the Jeep Man pulled a gun out from underneath his jacket. T.J. stood shocked and would have frozen like a statue if not for the continuous barking of the beast.

Ken must have come across guns before, because the sight of the steely weapon seemed to spark him to life. Ken started to creep up towards the Jeep Man, hoping that his concentration was focused on T.J. But as Ken walked over towards him, the beast turned its head and alerted its master.

The Jeep Man pulled the gun up and pointed it directly at Ken's face. Ken stood motionless as he looked down the barrel of the gun. But Ken must have been considering suicide because he started walking towards the Jeep Man again. Either he was insane or he did not believe the Jeep Man. This was Ken's first meeting with the Jeep Man. He did not know that this was no ordinary man who stood before him.

Ken, not caring, was now on his second step and was that much closer to the Jeep Man. The Jeep Man let him come a step closer and then cocked the gun and pointed it again at Ken. The realization that this was no game must have hit Ken, because he stopped dead in his tracks. Everyone stood motionless, waiting for the next move. T.J. and the beast were still in a stalemate. The Sullivan brothers had been frozen throughout the entire ordeal, and now Ken too was frozen and at the mercy of the Jeep Man.

Was this what the Jeep Man wanted all along? Would this be his ultimate victory? It looked like it might happen, but there was one obstacle stopping the Jeep Man. T.J. had his most prized possession and the man's only friend at his disposal. The Jeep Man looked at T.J. and signaled with a facial gesture for T.J. to leave. T.J. knew this was his opportunity to depart. It would seem as if the Jeep Man was trading their lives for the safety of his animal. T.J. walked back slowly as the other boys joined him. As they walked back, the Jeep Man still had his gun aimed at Ken. As they crept back further, the Jeep Man had a clear shot at them but chose to honor the silent agreement he and T.J. had made. There would be other battles. There would be other days. Time was on the Jeep Man's side, as he watched the boys disappear into the night.

As Jen finished her story, I listened in awe as she said, "And then T.J. and all of them left."

"Man, did I miss out!" I told Jen, disappointed. I had missed one of the greatest battles with the Jeep Man. It could have been my chance to challenge the Jeep Man one on one.

"You're lucky you weren't there. You probably would have gotten yourself killed," she said.

"This sucks," I said, angry at the hand fate dealt me.

"T.J. and them are lucky they didn't get shot," she said. "You guys should be more careful." Although I could hear her words, the message was lost to my excited ears. I said my good byes, as I went back inside the house and went up to my room. I sat on my bed and thought about today's events until I drifted asleep.

The next day, I had heard that T.J.'s mom had overheard a conversation concerning the lethal event. Nothing was more fierce that an angry lioness in fear for one of her cubs. So, T.J.'s mom went down to talk to the people in charge.

It appears that in the Jeep Man's early years as a security guard, a large number of men had ambushed him and beat him with large sticks. They did not stop until he lay unconscious. This was the only explanation that the people gave T.J.'s mom, and she told her son to keep a distance from the man from now on.

It was amazing to think that the Jeep Man had had adventures and other life occurrences outside of us. What had happened to bring him to this point in his life? Had he ever killed a man before? Had the slayer of children had a happy childhood? Had he ever been married? It just struck me that after all this time, we really knew nothing about our antagonist. In the past week, I had seen two different sides of the Jeep Man. I had seen a gentle Jeep Man and I had seen an evil fierce one. Which one was the real Jeep Man?

We were left with many questions without answers. Whatever his past was, it had led to us. Like an arranged marriage, we were wed to the Jeep Man till death do us part. I only wondered which one of us would come out the widow.

CHAPTER 12

The Canal

Clear skies had been dethroned by the gray ones which now reigned over the city. These black clouds hung about foretelling the events to come. The rainy season was now upon us. The sun had been taken prisoner by these clouds that now watched over us.

But this was not the typical rain we had seen in Moreno Valley. It had been raining extremely hard. The rain would come down in sheets, and you could hardly see ten feet in front of you. Days filled with tremendous rainfall plagued the city, and relief seemed far away. Certain streets of Moreno Valley ended up flooded, with the water reaching up to the door handles of some cars.

But the rain was not a curse for us all, for I loved the rainfall. While the city stayed warmly inside, I would go out and embrace the rain. I would splash through puddles. I would romp through the mud. I would stay outside and sing praises to the rain until my clothes were soaking wet. One day, I had even gotten to stay home from school since the streets were so badly flooded.

This Sunday morning was no different than the days that had preceded it. I had awakened to the sound of the rain hitting my window. If I had not known better, I would have assumed that someone was drenching my window with the outdoor hose. Now, at eleven o'clock, the rain had begun to show signs of letting up, at least for the moment. I sat at the kitchen table having my usual breakfast burrito while I stared out the window. The rain had come to a standstill, which had ruined my hopes for a little hail. I never had gotten the chance to play in a hailstorm and I figured that with the weather we had been having I might get my chance.

My vision was interrupted with a ring from the telephone. I picked it up and said, "Hello."

"Hey, Ian," said the voice, which I quickly recognized as Harold's. I was not very surprised. He always called on the weekends between eleven and twelve o'clock. "So what are you up to?"

"Just eatin' my breakfast," I told him while I took another bite out of my burrito. For the next ten minutes, Harold and I blathered on about our usual topic of the future adventures we all would have this summer.

"Man, I can't wait till summer time," Harold said.

"I know. It's gonna be so fun. You missed out on a lot of the stuff but at least you got to be here for the rest of 'em," I told Harold. I already had our summer mapped out. My favorite pastime during the school session was to plot out future quests. Day after day, I would boast to Harold of the previews of our summer blockbuster.

"First, we'll start searching for the cave up on ID. I've always known that there's a cave up there somewhere," I told him.

"Are you sure?" Harold asked.

"Yeah," I said confidently. "Once, when I was outside with Katie and Anna, we all saw some bats flying over our heads. So, I figure, that bats live in cave and the only place a cave can be is somewhere on our mountain."

"Wow!" he said in amazement. "You think there's anything in it?"

"I don't know," I told him. "But there's gotta be some good stuff."

"Wow, so what else are we gonna do?" he asked.

"Well, I also figure it's about time we get Dragon Lady. I kinda got a plan for her," I told Harold. "And then I want us to go diving in the swamp part of the lake. I got a feelin' that there's something down there. Then we gotta find that mountain lion that's up at ID, plus we also get to kick back the rest of the summer in the HIDJ." The HIDJ was the name of the boat I planned for the four of us to make. Each letter in the name stood for one of our first initials. In order, the letters stood for Harold, Ian, Dan and James. I had already drafted the designs and we would obtain the wood from stealing it from the construction area. "Trust me. I got a million things for us to do."

    I discussed topics ranging from Jeep Man strategy to hidden treasure upon the mountain. The conversation progressed until we reached the topic of what we would do today. Harold asked, "So what d'you wanna do?"

    "I don't know. I guess you can come over and play video games since it's raining outside," I said as my eyes drifted out the window. Then, an idea popped into my head. "I know what we can do, Harold."

    "What?" he asked.

    "Well, you know how its been raining hard?" I asked.

    "Yah," he said.

    "And you know how the streets have all been flooding?" I asked, trying to give him a hint.

    "Well, if the streets have been all flooded, I bet the canal is super flooded. It'll be as deep as a pool, and we can go swimming and stuff," I told him. Then when we're finished we can go up to ID and have mud fights.

    "That sounds cool," Harold said.

    "Come over to my house, and we'll get the stuff we need," I told him. "Wear your old stuff, so you won't mess up your clothes"

    "Okay, I'll be over there in a few minutes. See ya," Harold said, as he hung up the phone.

    My mind raced with images of the flooded canal. This was going to be remarkable. I ran upstairs into my bedroom and searched the wreckage otherwise known as my closet for my

Halloween outfit. I bulldozed through the closet, throwing out clothes and toys onto the floor. After a few minutes of digging, I finally found it. It was the plastic robe I had worn last year for Halloween. It was supposed to resemble the robe of a monk. Since it was plastic, it would keep the rain off me, and it even had a hood to keep the water out of my face.

This was fine for me, but Harold too had to be kept dry. After a few minutes of thought while I put on some old rags, I ran back downstairs and picked up an empty trash bag. I then took a pair of scissors from the kitchen drawer and cut three large holes into the trash bag, one for his head and the other two for his arms.

About two minutes later, I heard a knock on the door and instantly knew who it was. "I got it!" I yelled as I ran to the door. I did not want my mom to get up and get suspicious. My mom would not let me even go out in the rain, let alone go in the canal. I opened the door to see Harold a little drenched from the rain. After saying hi, I joined him outside so there would be no chance of my mom over hearing. "I just finished making you this rain coat," I said as I handed him the trash bag. He looked it over for a few seconds, and then slid it over his head and put it on. "That'll keep the rain off you."

"I forgot to bring some old shoes," Harold said. "My mom'll kill me if I get these shoes messed up."

"I don't think I have any more old shoes that'll fit you," I told him. I thought a few seconds and then said, "We can use some plastic bags to put over our shoes. That way they won't get wet or muddy." I ran back into the house and came out with a couple of rubber bands and two plastic bags from the grocery store. Harold slipped the bags over his feet and then I slid the rubber bands over his feet and around his ankles. "There, that'll hold 'em."

"Is that everything?" Harold asked anxiously.

"Yah, that should about do it," I said. "Let me just go and tell my mom." I walked back over, opened the door a crack and yelled, "I'm going over to Harold's." I heard no response and decided to take that as an approval to go. I then slipped on my plastic robe, walked back over to Harold and said, "Ok, let's go."

We left my house and headed down Guajome. The rain had started up again, but we did not pay it much attention. After years of playing in the rain, it had become as common to me as the air. So we walked down the street, taking a shortcut straight through the Jeep Man's territory. On a rainy day like this, we were guaranteed safe haven and walked straight through the area without any hassles. From there, we hopped the fence and made our way towards the canal.

"This is going to be fun," I told Harold.

"I know. I can't wait till we're in the water," Harold said.

"You'd just better be careful," I said. "Remember, you can't swim that good." Whenever we were at the recreation center and were playing in the pool, Harold was forced to stay in the shallow end or he had to hold onto the edge to the pool while we played in the deep end. At best, he could stay afloat for about three seconds before he started to sink.

"Ah, I can swim good," Harold said in protest.

"Yah, that's why Michael beat you in the pool," I told him. Michael was the four-year-old neighborhood Dennis the Menace who had humiliated Harold in a swimming race earlier this summer.

"I could have beat him if I wanted to, I was just bein' nice," Harold said.

"Sure, Harold," I said sarcastically.

"I forgot to tell you guys, but before I moved over here I was on the swim team and I was real good," he said. This was particular amazing since the only stroke Harold knew was the doggie paddle, but by now I was accustomed to Harold's gigantic fibs, and shrugged them off like annoying gnats.

We walked for about five more minutes until we crossed the field and reached the sidewalk, preparing to cross the street. I turned to Harold, pointed in front of us and said, "Wow, would you look at that!" The streets were flooded with water. We watched cars drive by going through the water that covered three quarters of their tires.

"If the streets are like this just imagine what the canal is like!" said Harold.

"I know. Let's hurry up and go," I said as Harold and I stepped into the water. It rose up to my shin and felt remarkably cold. We ran through as quickly as we could, laughing the entire way. It was extremely tiring. We splashed frantically as we crossed the street, kicking water up into our faces. Once we crossed, we stood on the sidewalk trying to catch our breath, wiping the water off our faces.

"That was fun," I said in between my gasps for air.

"Yah, sure was," Harold said as he gazed upon the fence that enclosed the canal. It was still about twenty feet away, but that made it better because we would be out of sight of onlookers driving by. Filled with excitement and a new burst of energy, we sprinted over to the fence.

We took the long way around, using an old, abandoned street to get to the canal. The street had been fenced off so that no cars could use the road, but there were so many tears in the fence that a boy could easily walk through. After walking down the street, we made our way through the dirt and tumbleweeds, which separated the old street from the canal.

The canal was on the opposite side of the street from our mountain. The canal stretched down a couple of miles. Usually the canal was bare, resembling an empty pool, but when filled, the canal would take the water underneath the street into a tunnel which was laced with bars. This way, no big objects could pass through, and then like a waterfall, the water would run into the swampy part of the lake.

We walked up to the second fence that surrounded the canal. I gave it a good scan. I turned to Harold, and with a smile I said, "This is gonna be even easier than I thought. There's no barbed wire or anything to keep us out." As I finished my sentence, I noticed in the distance a car which seemed to be driving unusually slowly. "Come on, let's go down further so no cars can see us."

"All right," Harold said, as we started to walk away from the nearby streets.

We walked along the fence until I felt satisfied and said, "Ok, this should be a good spot."

After staring at the fence for about a minute, Harold looked at me and said, "So what now?"

"I guess we climb it," I said. I jumped on the fence and began to climb it. Although my hands were a little numb from the cold, the climb was fairly easy. When I reached out my hand to grab the top of the fence, the wire pierced the palms of my hands. "Ow!" I yelled as I let go and fell back to the ground. Searing pain was now flowing through my hands.

"What happened?" Harold asked stopping his climb.

"The top of that fence cut me," I said as I blew on my hands hoping to soothe my pain. Harold continued on his climb, probably thinking that I had picked a bad spot, but when he reached the top, I watched as he yelled in pain and fell, joining me on the ground. I placed my hand in the mud and let the coldness of the mud help numb the pain. "Put your hands in the mud. It makes 'em feel better." Harold put his hands in the mud as we both gained some temporary relief.

We then sat in the mud and rain for about two minutes before Harold turned to me and said, "So what do we do now?"

"I don't know," I said as I thought to myself. This was obviously the reason they had not put barbed wire on the fence.

The wires at the top of the fence had been sharpened like a blade. After thinking a bit more, I stood up and said, "We can put our jackets on the top of the fence and have it covering the sharp stuff. Then we'll just climb over our jackets instead of the sharp stuff."

"Good thinking," Harold said.

I took off my robe and laid it onto the ground. Then I took off the jacket I had been wearing underneath the robe and put it on top of the fence. "All right, let me see yours," I said as I stuck out my hand. Harold took off the trash bag he had been wearing and threw it on the ground. He then unzipped his jacket and handed it over to me. I took it and then laid it on top of my jacket. "That ought to do it."

I started to climb, knowing my plan would work. But once I reached the top, the wire, like a needle, went through the jackets and into my skin again. Not wanting to start over, I tried to block the pain out of my mind. As quickly as I could, I began to muster all my upper body strength and then used it to lift my legs over the fence like a high jumper; I threw myself completely over the fence. I landed hard on my hips, but if there was any pain going through my hips I quickly forgot it due to the pain that was going through my hands.

I jumped up and down moaning, as I quickly remembered the remedy and put my hands in the mud. As the pain subsided, I turned to Harold and said, "Ok, you go."

"You want me to do that?" Harold asked.

"Yah," I said, pausing for a second. "But before you go, throw me over that piece of wood." Next to Harold lay a long piece of wood, which had probably been left by some careless trucker.

Harold walked up to it, picked it up and threw it over the fence. "What are you gonna use that for?" he asked as the wood hit the ground.

I walked over to it, picked it up and said, "I'm going to see how deep the water is."

"I'll be over there in a second," he said as he started to climb the fence.

Although I could not see it yet, the canal roared like a raging river. I walked up to the edge of the canal and began walking down it toward the water with the wood in my hand. The wood would make an excellent ruler since it was a little over ten feet long. But once my old, worn-out shoes hit the wet cement of the canal, the grip on my shoes became nonexistent and I lost my balance. As I fell to the ground, I dropped the piece of wood. It landed against the wall of the canal and then bounced into the rapids below. The cement of the wall was so slippery that once I hit the ground I began sliding towards the water.

"Harold!" I yelled out for help as I slowly slid toward the water. Panicking, I used the palms of my hands as brakes. My body slid a bit more as I ground my hand into the cement. Luckily, I stopped within a few feet of the water. This had not been a good day for my hands - they burned like fire. From the distance, I could see the strong current sweeping the wood away towards the lake. It bobbed up and down and then vanished underneath the street.

"What's up?" Harold asked.

"Nothing," I said, still a little rattled. "Just hurry up and get over here." Slowly, I began crawling back up, making sure to keep my balance. Once at the top, I sat on the edge and stared out into the water. I watched as the choppy water roared by. I began to wonder how deep it was. Could we stand in it? Could the water be crossed?

My thoughts were broken up as Harold yelled, "Ian, help!" I turned my head to see Harold's body stuck on the top of the fence. His body straddled the fence like a man on a horse. I could only imagine the pain Harold was going through, as the wires were doing a number on his body as he moaned in pain.

"Just hold on," I yelled as ran over to him. Not having time to think, I picked up his body with my bare hands, lifting him off the sharp wires. I elevated him high over my head, carried him to safety and then threw him to the ground.

Harold lay on the ground for a little bit and then sat up and said, "Thanks."

"Did that hurt?" I asked

"Heck, yah," he said. "The jackets were underneath me, so that helped a bit."

"When we're finished, we'll find another way to get over that fence. We're not going through that again," I told him. "So are you ready?"

"Yah," he said.

"Wait here for a bit and let me see how deep it is," I told him. Harold nodded and I began walking down the side of the canal again. This time I took extremely slow steps and I did not have the wood to worry about. I crept up to the edge of the water, and took a long, deep breath as I braced myself for the contact with the water. I sat down and used my legs and feet to slowly crawl into the water.

The touch of the water to my skin sent shivers throughout my body. This was the coldest water I had ever felt. The amazing or foolish thing was that I kept putting more of my body into it. First my feet, then my ankles, and then my legs were submerged in the water. Before I knew it, I was standing at the bottom of the canal with the water an inch or two above my waist. I gritted my teeth as the water was so cold it hurt. I looked up at Harold and yelled, "Come on in. It's not that deep."

The lower half of my body started to numb and the water seemed to be getting less painful. The current was incredible. The water pushed against me so hard, I felt as if I was walking through a hurricane. I felt as if I could fall at any moment. Of course, this was not an option. Further ahead, where the canal took the water into the lake, there were bars which kept out large debris. If we were to fall and get taken to the bars we would be trapped underwater.

Not waiting for Harold, I began trying to cross the canal. Now, I was in the middle of the canal when Harold had just gotten in. I do not know how he could stand; the water only reached above my waist, but it reached up to Harold's chest. "How're you doing?" I asked him.

"O...o.k.," he stuttered, the cold seeming to affect his voice.

"Just make sure you don't slip or anything," I yelled. I kept crossing. My legs now were so numb it was getting hard to control them. My legs felt like they had been shot with Novacain. My head began spinning and my only thoughts were to reach the other side. Finally, I felt the curve of the wall and began climbing out of the water. I sat down on the canal in pain, as feeling began returning to my legs. My legs burned as if they were on fire. As I lay back in pain, Harold crawled up beside me and sat down.

"The water hurts," he said as he sat next to me.

"I know. My legs are killing me," I told him. We sat back and recuperated for a couple of minutes. Then Harold sat up and said, "What are we gonna do now?"

"We'll wait here until we're o.k. again. Then we go back and finish crossing the canal," I told him. We waited, and after about five minutes had passed, we got up and started our way across the canal. On all fours like infants, we crawled backwards with our feet first going into the water. Side by side, we entered the frigid water. We crawled backward until we had hit the ground and began crossing the canal. My body tired quickly as it walked against the tremendous current. With my body frozen, my mind wandered and I imagined myself at home in my warm bath. Hopefully, my mom had bought soap to make a bubble bath. The bath was only about an hour away. Then all of a sudden, Harold yelled, "Help!" I turned my head to see Harold losing his balance and falling in the water. Harold's body fell back towards the water.

    I went towards him. My body felt like it was moving in slow motion. He waved his arms into the air, as his body was about to hit he water. I reached my hand out and grabbed his arm. His body went into the water, pulling me in a little. I managed to keep my balance and hold onto him, keeping his head out of the water. I stood up and pulled him up with me. Harold looked over and said in a dreary voice, "Thanks again."

    "Let's hurry up and go home," I said. This time, I kept a grip on his shirt as we finished crossing the canal. Once we were out of the water, we crawled all the way up onto the dirt.

    Once at the top, Harold looked at me and said, "I'm too tired to climb over that fence."

    "Me too," I agreed. "Come on. Let's find another way," We stood up and walked alongside the fence for about five minutes.

    "What are we stopping for?" Harold asked.

    "That's how we'll get to the other side," I told him as I pointed to a hole underneath the fence.

    "That's not gonna fit us," Harold said.

    "When we dig it, it will," I said. We kneeled on the ground and used our hands to dig away the dirt. Just as I had expected, the ground had been softened by the rain. In a matter of seconds, we had a wide enough hole to fit our bodies.

    "Is that it?" he asked.

    "That should do it," I told him. "Now start crawling." Harold crawled through the hole, getting himself a bit muddy, but making it with ease. I soon followed. I had a tighter squeeze than Harold, but I made it through nevertheless.

We were finally finished and ready to go home. We walked down and grabbed our jackets and our plastic raincoats. We walked for a couple of minutes on the dirt till we reached the sidewalk and started to make our way home.

About halfway home, the two of us heard a strange noise, which seemed to be following us. We looked around, but could not see anything. About a minute later, Harold started to laugh as he pointed down at my shoes. Half my sock was coming out of a small hole on the bottom of my shoes. The sound we heard had been the sound of my sock slapping the pavement. I looked at Harold and joined him in laughter. Despite the rain, the cold, the exhaustion and the pain, the sound of the slap against the pavement kept us laughing the entire way home.

CHAPTER 13

Grave Digging

What to do? The eternal question that has plagued kids on boring days now haunted me. It was Saturday morning, and there was not a soul in sight. James was off on some church function. Dan was playing in a basketball game for the Moreno Valley league and Harold had gone to the local mall with his mother. I sat in my room wondering what I would do today, for to waste a precious Saturday was like throwing away good food.

I rummaged through the sea of comic books on my floor hoping to find something to relieve my boredom. Once I finished with the rummaging, I picked up my selected comics and lay down on my bed. Then, after reading a few issues of Batman, X-men and a few other titles, I went over to the phone and tried calling Dan to see if he was home yet. But after dialing the number, there was no answer.

I paced back and forth in my room. The boredom was driving me insane. I climbed up on my bed and gazed out of the window. The sky was blue, the clouds were few, and the temperature was around seventy degrees. I could not waste a day like this.

To make it even worse, my Dad had left for work before I had woken up. This meant I had no chores. I had a perfectly free day, and I was wasting it, procrastinating in my room.

I went downstairs into the kitchen and opened the refrigerator. I pulled out a slice of cheese and quickly devoured it. My mom sat on the couch watching some fashion program on television. I gazed out the backyard window. It was torturous having to be confined inside. I looked up at ID mountain. ID was the new name of our hill. It stood for Ian and

Dan. The hill had been renamed after the tales of Dan and myself spending the night up there.

This was the best time of year to go hiking up ID. Due to all the rain we had had recently, the entire mountain had shed its summer coat of dry brushes for the winter coat of green fertilization. Harold and I had even found a small waterfall that ran alongside the mountain.

Staring at ID got me a little anxious for a quick hike. I did not want to go up without the others, but who knew how long it would be till they returned. After staring at the carpet for two minutes, I decided not to wait and to go up there without them. Hopefully, there would still be plenty of mud and puddles to thrash around in. When it rained hard, large puddles formed around the base of the mountain. Some even reached widths around 30 feet.

I ran upstairs to find some old clothes I could wear to thrash around in the mud. I'd sooner face the Dragon Lady then have my mom catch me mudding up some of my good clothes. I put on an old T-shirt and an even older pair of shoes and headed out the door.

As the door slammed shut, an idea leaped into my head. This was the kind of idea Einstein had before he concluded that 'E equals mc squared. It was so simplistic it made me angry I had not thought of it sooner. When I went up to the mountain, I would retrieve the piece of wood we had carved our names into.

Before, when we had gone to the mountain together for the first time, T.J. and his little brother Corey had hidden it. It was somewhere on top of the huge boulder next to the split rock. Hopefully, It would not take long to find and retrieve it. Then, I could spend the rest of the day wallowing and swimming in the mud.

I congratulated myself on my enormous intellect as I left my driveway and headed down Guajome. So off I went, down

Guajome, through the Jeep Man's territory, past the school, along the lake and finally to the mountain. I walked past the base of the mountain, noticing the large puddles that had formed. I then walked over to the main trail. It all looked spectacular. ID was layered with green grass except for the boulders and a few of the trails. I walked up the path amazed at the beautiful scenery.

    Walking up the mountain made me reminisce about one of my old grand schemes. I planned to map out the entire mountain. With the immensity of the mountain, there were too many trails and too many key points that could be forgotten. And even though I had spent years upon the mountain, most of it lay unexplored. Since school was in session, I did not have enough time at the moment to implement my idea, but once glorious summer came, I could start the project. It might take the whole summer, or it might even take two summers. Either option thrilled me.

    As I continued to ponder my future plans, I walked up the main trail, getting closer to the top of our hill. Then suddenly, I stopped dead in my tracks as I felt my heart stop. My eyes bulged out and my body felt limp as I stared in front of me. I stood motionless as a bead of sweat rolled along my forehead, down my nose and then dropped to the ground. A million unfathomable thoughts raced through my head as I gazed upon this momentous surprise.

    Before me, on this very spot that we had hiked upon a million times, there was now a grave. There was a large wooden cross which reached up to my chest. The work on the cross was not a shoddy job. Whoever had built it definitely had taken their time. The cross was made up of two extremely thick pieces of wood, which would have been tough for one man to carry up the hill by himself. At the base of the cross, there were large stones the size of grapefruits formed in a rectangular shape. The rectangle was big enough to fit a large animal or a small man. The thought of it sent tingles along my spine. On the neck of the cross was a loop of string, which could have been used as a necklace for someone.

My legs trembled as I walked closer to the gravesite. I stood just outside the grave, making sure not to cross over the rocks which encircled the grave. Who knew what unlucky omens I could unleash on myself by crossing that barrier? My body felt numb. My mind was confused. I looked down at the grave hoping it would unleash some sort of meaning to these chains of event.

But instead of illumination, I felt something even worse. On the ground lying in the center of the grave lay a used bullet shell. I stared at it for about thirty seconds. What did this mean? What was buried underneath here? I began to feel extremely alone and wished that Dan and the others were here.

I knew what I had to do. I left the gravesite and walked over to the split boulder, and then turned to face the huge boulder which lay next to it. I used broken chunks of the huge boulder as steps and proceeded to climb up it. Once at the top of the boulder, I looked out upon the city. But I didn't have time to admire the view. I used the height advantage to make sure no one was following me, and then started to look for the wood. I found a huge crevice on the top of the boulder, which had to have been the hole T.J. said he hid the wood in. I peered into the crevice, but I couldn't see anything due to the darkness.

I then placed my hand into it and felt around. All I could fell was the stone of the boulder and a few insects crawling around. I stretched my hand even further. This time my fingers ran along something. With a small tug, it pulled out easily, and to my delight, it was the carving. I looked at it and was surprised to see it still in good condition. Luckily, T.J. had it well hidden, which must of also helped to preserve it. I could still clearly read: 'Ian Corey Dan T.J. James July 7, 1991.'

My plan had worked and a feeling of comfort rushed over me. Earlier I had felt frightened by the feeling of loneliness that had overtaken me. I climbed down the boulder, being extra careful not to slip since now I was using one hand to hold the carving. Once on the ground, I clung tightly to the carving as I made my way past the grave. I made sure to keep the carving in front as I used it as a sort of protective shield while I walked past the morbid place. I took one more glance back and then started on my way home and went down the main trail. This whole experience was too much for me. "What should I do? I wish the other guys were here," I thought to myself.

Feelings ranging from morbid curiosity to deathly terror ran through me. It was a long walk home as I continually debated the meaning of the morbid sight. After getting home from the mountain, I sat in my room unable to forget the events that had transpired. The thought which I had tried to purge from my mind popped into my head. What could be underneath the grave? Was it some beast that had been put out of its misery or was it a person who had had a tragic accident? And even worse, why would someone bury any creature up top the mountain? Was it accidental or intentional? Perhaps it was just a senior prank from one of the nearby schools. Perhaps there was nothing under the grave but dirt.

But why then, was there a bullet shell there? It had to have meant something. And what did the rope necklace have to do with all this? Maybe it did involve foul play. If it did, what if the person responsible had seen me at the gravesite? What if he had followed me home? I stared outside my window as I continued to think to myself.

Over the next few minutes, as my fear began to subside, an idea came into my head. I then became extremely excited, for this would be the greatest adventure of them all. A smile began to grow on my face. I jumped off the bed and ran to the telephone. The greatest adventure was right in front of me.

With a few quick calls, I rounded up the guys and within the next ten minutes Harold and I were in the Farabelli garage sitting in a circle, prepared for discussion. James came over and sat down and said, "I tried calling Dan again, but he wasn't home,"

"All right, well, we'll have to start without him," I said.

"So what's the deal?" James asked.

"Yah," Harold said, echoing James' question.

"Well, I was up at the mountain earlier today, and I was looking for that carving that we made a long time ago," I told them.

"You mean that one that me you Dan, and T.J. made," James said referring to the carved piece of wood.

"Yah, that one," I said.

"What wood?" Harold asked.

"Well, a while ago, we all went hiking on the mountain, We had a piece of wood with us and all of us carved our names into it. Then we hid it," I said explaining it to Harold.

"Oh," he said ,acknowledging the importance of the wood.

"So what's the big deal about that?" James asked.

"The wood's not the big thing. When I was up there looking for it, I found something else," I told them.

"What'd you find?" Harold said.

"A grave," I said. They stared at me in disbelief.

"A grave?" Harold asked.

"Are you joking?" James asked.

"No, it's for real," I said, validating my statement. James and Harold's mouth dropped.

"Wow," Harold mumbled. "What'd it look like?"

"Well, there was this big wooden cross and it came up about this high," I said as I pointed to my chest. "Then there were these big rocks that went around the grave."

"Daaaaang," said Harold in amazement.

"So what did you do?" James asked.

"I don't know," I said, trying to recall my feelings during the situation. "I just went up and got the wood, then left."

"Man, I bet that it was pretty scary," Harold said.

"I haven't even told you the scariest part," I told them.

"How could it get any scarier?" Harold asked.

"There was a bullet shell lying right on top – right in the middle," I told them.

"Really?" James asked.

"Yah, really," I told him. "And then there was this rope thing that looked like it could have been someone's necklace."

"What do you think happened?" James asked.

"I'm not sure," I told him.

"Do you think someone's dead up there?" he asked.

"I don't know. It could just be a dead animal or it might be nothing that's up there," I told him.

"Wow, man. That's crazy," James said, still stunned.

"I know," Harold said, sharing James' emotions.

"But that's not why I called you guys," I told them. Both of them threw puzzled looks at me.

"If that's not it, then what is?" James asked.

"Well..." I said, pausing for a little bit.

"Just say it," James said eagerly.

"We're going to go up there and dig it up," I said.

"What?" James and Harold asked simultaneously. They then turned and looked at each other in disbelief.

"We're going to dig it up?" Harold asked.

"Yep," I said.

"The grave?" Harold asked, making sure I had not confused my words.

"Yah, the grave," I said. They both took in long deep breaths.

James looked up at me and said, "You want us to go and do this tonight?"

"Not tonight," I said.

"When?" asked Harold.

"Well, since this Saturday is Halloween, I figured we could do it on the night before. This way it'll make it real spooky," I told them as I watched their faces still in disbelief.

After a few seconds of collecting themselves, James asked, "Are you sure you want to do this?"

"Yah, it'll be cool," I said.

"On the night before Halloween?" Harold asked.

"Yah," I told them.

"But who knows what'll be out there on the night before Halloween?" Harold said.

"I know. That's what'll make it better," I told him.

As shocked as they were, they knew my decision was final. When it came to adventures, I could be as stubborn as a mule. James looked over to me and said, "So we're going to do this, this Friday?"

"Yep," I said.

"I have football practice," James said.

"We'll just go after words," I said. "That'll make it even better cause then it'll be night and stuff."

"This is going to be so crazy," James said.

"I know. This'll be the best adventure yet," I told them. Then the three of us began going over the plans for that Friday night. We spent the rest of the afternoon going over details, until we each got hungry and went home for dinner.

Then, as the weekend ended and the school days started up once again, I would find myself during the day straining to pay attention. It was harder that usual to listen to the mundane lectures, for while the drones sat patiently jotting down every word, I sat fidgeting in my chair dreaming of the day when I would become the greatest adventure of all. While they walked throughout the halls discussing the pointless gossip of whether Jennifer kissed Chris, I dreamed of obtaining my ultimate prize. It was fitting, for by the time Halloween passed, I would have destroyed my ultimate fear. My chance to meet death face to face had arrived. All my questions would be answered. All my fears would be laid to rest.

But my excitement seemed only to prolong the waiting as the days dragged by ever so slowly. Day after day passed as I writhed in boredom waiting for Friday to come, until I finally found myself lying in bed with just a few hours separating me from my ultimate goal. I lay in bed staring at the ceiling wondering what tomorrow might bring. Was this what I had been searching for all along? Were all the answers I needed right under my nose? All my questions, my fears, my hopes and dreams were about to become realized.

CHAPTER 14

The Cure

It seemed all of death's allies were gone. Time was my unwitting slave, as it would be forced to let me know all of its secrets. And as time brought me closer to my destiny, I nodded off to sleep envisioning what mysteries tomorrow would bring me.

I awoke the next day and went to school like usual. The day had dragged by like the days preceding it; except for once, I was extremely excited throughout the day. I would watch the clock tick ever so slowly. It did not bother me though; time could play its little games, but it would inevitably have to send me to my destiny. Class after class passed as the day began to fade. Then lunch came, and then more classes until the day was finally over. I got a ride from one of the girls who also lived in Moreno Valley and before I knew it I was finally home.

I skipped to the front door, unlocked it and went inside. After drinking a glass of orange juice, I started to search the house for the garage key. As I looked underneath the living room couch, I heard a knock at the door. Already knowing who it was, I ran to the door, opened it and saw a wet Harold standing outside.

"Hey, Harold," I told him.

"Hey, Ian," he said.

"Are you ready?" I asked him.

"Yah, I thought it'd never get here. Today was going super slow," he told me.

"I know, me too," I said. "I'm just glad the waiting is over."

"But you know it's raining outside?" he asked.

"That's even better," I said. "Just think of how cool its going to be go up at night and do it in the rain. Did you eat?"

"No," he said.

"Well, let's eat now, cause we need to take care of some stuff so we can be ready when James and Dan come home," I told him. We went inside and munched on some chips and drank soda until we were full. After putting the food and drinks away and finding the garage key on top of the microwave, Harold and I headed out the front door and over to the garage. I unlocked it and opened up the door. We scoured through the wreckage hoping to find one of my shovels.

After ten minutes of searching, we found one, and I said, "Ok, we'll use this one and then maybe we'll get another one from James' house."

"There's a shovel at my house," Harold said.

"Ok, that might be better," I told him. "That way we'll be even more ready when he's home." We took the shovel out of the garage and closed the garage door. I laid the shovel down on the ground; then both of us headed over to his house. It was sprinkling the entire way there, and by the time we arrived we were soaked. Luckily, his mom was not there, so we would not run into any trouble.

After searching the garage for a while, we found the shovel and started to head back to Guajome. The entire way, we talked of the adventure coming up. "This is gonna be pretty cool," I told Harold.

"I know, I can't wait," he said.

"Well, James should be home within the hour," I said.

"So what do you think's up there?" Harold asked.

"I don't know, but whatever it is, it should be pretty neat," I said, trying to sound enthusiastic, but I was not sure what to feel. How should a boy feel when the point that determines his very existence is a couple of hours away?

And as I pondered these strange feelings, we headed back to Guajome with the rain now coming down harder. Once we made it back home, we waited around the side of the house.

figuring since we were already wet there was no reason to get dry and then get wet all over again. So, we stood in the rain eagerly awaiting James' arrival and trying not to look suspicious.

Then in the next hour, as the sun went down, James' car finally pulled up. With James' family piling out of the car, we ran across the street, leaving the shovels behind so we would not arouse any suspicion. "Hey, James," Harold said as we walked up to him. There was a boy who I had never seen before standing next to him. I looked at James with a puzzled look. I hope he was not bailing from this adventure.

"Ian, this is my friend Johnathin. He has to spend the night tonight," he told me. I looked at James, a little disappointed. "But it's cool. I told him what we were going to do and he's going to come up with us."

I looked the boy over. He was a black kid about average weight and size who was around James' age. He looked a little too clean-cut, and I did not like bringing someone new in to join us. I would hate to bring him up there and have him crack under the pressure. But if this is what it took to get James to come, then so be it. "It's all right with me," I said. "We just need to hurry up and get down there before it gets too late and our parents don't let us go outside."

"What should we do first?" James asked.

"We've already got shovels," Harold said.

"We'll need a flashlight," I told James.

"Ok, I'll go get it. When I'm in there I'm gonna change my clothes," he said as he and Johnathin went inside the house.

"Wait here, Harold. I'm going to go in and call Dan," I said as I went inside, leaving Harold to keep the vigil. As I went inside the house, I passed James and Johnathin, who were going to the garage. I went to the phone and dialed Dan's number.

"Hello," Dan said, answering the phone.

"Hey, it's me," I said.

"Hey, Ian, what's up?" he asked.

"We're getting ready to go and we need you to hurry up and meet us at James' house," I told him.

"Ian," Dan said in an all too familiar shaky voice. "I don't think I'm gonna be able to make it."

"What do you mean you can't make it?" I asked him.

"I have this game Monday, and I don't want to get pneumonia or any thing," Dan said.

I had to give Dan credit. That was one of his better excuses. Not admitting it though, I said, "That's the lamest thing I ever heard."

"And my parents are home, and they'd never let me out in this rain," Dan said.

"Well, duh," I said mocking him. "Of course they're not gonna let you out and dig up some dead body. You tell them something made up."

"This game's really important and I don't want to be sick for it," Dan said, trying to think of anything that would get himself out of this.

"All right," I said frustrated. "I'll talk to you later." With James' parents walking about, I did not have time to talk Dan into going. After hanging up the phone, I met James and Johnathin with the flashlight.

"Is Dan coming?" James asked.

"You know Dan," I told him. "That chicken's stayin' home. You guys ready?" They nodded their heads and with that we headed out the front door and over to Harold's. Once there, the four of us walked across the street, picked up the shovels and headed down Guajome. It was completely dark now and the rain was coming down thunderously. The only good thing about it was that not even the Jeep Man would be out in this weather.

Luckily, the rain was also a distraction from the way I was feeling. I was only less than an hour away from an event that was so powerful, it would change my life forever. The banter of my comrades also seemed to take my mind off these cosmic matters. I listened as we walked across the field and James said, "This rain is horrible."

"I can't believe you guys are doing this," said Johnathin.

"We do stuff like this all the time," Harold said.

"You get used to it," I said, but just as I finished my sentence, my right foot lodged into the mud. And when I lifted my leg, my shoe stayed firmly planted into the ground. We all stared at my exposed foot sitting in the mud and then looked back at my shoe stuck in the mud.

We exploded in laughter for the next minute until our sides were too sore to laugh any more. I put my foot back in my shoe and laced them up extremely tight, and pulled with a great degree of strength to free my shoe from the sludge. Once done, we started on the journey again, and James said, "This is worse than going through a swamp." Due to the heavy rain, the ground had given way and had been transformed into some sort of sludge that covered the whole field.

Of course, this made our journey more difficult. The mud rose past our ankles and it felt as if we were walking through an inch of snow. "My legs our getting tired," Harold said.

"I know, me too, but we gotta keep going," I told him

"This is pretty bad, Ian," James said of the weather.

"Yeah, but we don't got a choice," I said as we trudged on further. Then the four of us with our aching legs finally reached the end of the field and walked upon the sidewalk.

"Glad that's over," James said.

"Yeah, me too," I told him. Our legs were covered in mud, and not one spot on our clothing was dry. We headed across the flooded street, where the high rising water washed off some of the mud on our legs. Once there, we walked past the canal, listening to the roar of the water as we crossed the street over to the base of the mountain.

We all stood and stared at the top of ID. I looked at them and said, "Let's get goin'." We started walking up towards the mountain. We took the usual path where we walked along the lake, around the gorge and up the base of the mountain. After a long walk, we reached the main trail. With a glance at each other, we headed up the main trail as my pulse slightly quickened. I felt as if I had gained superhuman hearing. I could hear the sound of my heart beating and each footstep taken by the others. It seemed like we were moving in slow motion as I watched my friends tread up the mountain.

After climbing halfway up the trail, James said, "Are you sure there's something up here? I don't see anything."

"Trust me," I told him, still trying to adjust my senses. My body shook with nervousness.

"I don't see anything, Ian. I'd hate to have come up all this way for..." James said, not being able to finish his complaint. The four of us stood in awe. It was the most awesome sight I had seen in my entire life. We could see the black outline of the cross with the moonlight shedding a bit of light on it. The rain had created a mist on top of the mountain that seemed to hang behind the cross. It was spectacular.

The four of us walked over to the gravesite. Except for the sound of rain hitting the dirt, there was silence as the four of us spread out and encircled the grave. "See, just like Ian said," Harold told James.

We all stared down upon the gravesite and watched the bullet shell wiggle due to the heavy rain. James looked over to me and said, "What now?"

I trembled in fear as I tried to muster up some courage. This was just death's way of keeping me from its door. I looked up at James and said, "Let's get started." James lurched over and picked up the bullet shell. After looking at it for a second, James set it aside. The four of us stood there: James and I held the shovels, Harold had the flashlight and Johnathin stood mesmerized by the grave.

We all stood around waiting for someone to make the first move. Seeing that all eyes were upon me, I stared down at the grave, raised my shovel, and drove it into the dirt, piercing death's skin. James' shovel then hit the ground as we proceeded to dig up the grave. I dug with an intense focus, for I was digging for the very secrets of my life. I had turned the tables on death, for now I was the stalker.

As I continued to dig with a great vigor, James and I piled the dirt as we started to make some headway. Harold continued providing the light for us while Johnathin had begun whimpering as he stared in horror. I knew there would be problems with bringing an untrained kid on such an important mission. It did not matter though, as we continued to dig, getting even further.

Then James' shovel struck something and we all heard a loud clang. I stopped shoveling. Harold came in and brought the light a little closer. My moment had arrived. I reached my hand to the ground hoping to touch death's face. I put my fingers into the ground and let them run across the substance. It was solid. There was definitely something there. Using both my hands, I dug around it and then began pulling it out using both my hands. I pulled the object out, brushed the dirt off it and said, "It's just a rock." The others sighed in relief.

I renewed my digging with a new intensity when Johnathin, with tears streaming down his face, cried out, "I want to go home."

"We're almost finished," I said, trying to reassure him.

"I just want to go home," Johnathin whimpered. I ignored his cries and began digging once again. I was so close to death I could taste it.

"Please, let me go home!" Johnathin cried.

"Maybe we should," James suggested.

"But we're so close," I told him.

"Look at those rocks over there," he said pointing at a nearby boulder. We looked to see the rock marked with some weird type of marking. "I learned about stuff like that in Sunday school. Those could be satanic marks."

I did not care. The devil himself would not keep me from my prize. I started to dig with the ferocity of a man digging for his freedom. I repeatedly plunged the shovel in and out of the ground, ignoring the pain that had been building in my right shoulder. I threw the shovel down and used my own hands to dig. Like a dog digging up a bone, I plowed through the ground. As I dug, I could not get Johnathin's weeping out of my mind.

I looked at the others and realized James had set his shovel down. I knew I was wrong. I had been using the others for my quest. But I had to find the great mystery, and I was so close, and I had waited so long.

Then I looked over at Harold and James and thought of T.J. and Dan. I had had the greatest moments of my life with these four. I considered them brothers. They meant more to me than anything. But my quest was so close to coming to an end and the mysteries of death could be just a few minutes away. I weighed in my mind what was more important - discovering death's shrouded secret or my friends' well-being.

The decision was easy. I looked at the others and said, "Let's go home." James lent me a hand and helped pull me out of the hole. James and I pushed some of the dirt, which was now mud, back into the whole. If there was anything buried underneath this mountain, it would be left to rest in peace.

"Come on. If we hurry we can get back before our parents suspect anything."

So we left the mountain and the secrets it held and made our way back home. Later on that night, I lay in bed trying to make sense of all of it. I was still as scared of death as before, but now it wasn't the most important aspect of my life. My friends and the adventures we had shared were more important to me that my ghastly crusade. Death had become secondary.

And now I had even become grateful for my fear. I knew now that was what kept me grounded. My fear was why I saw things differently than the norm. It was why I took advantage of life while others were content to have life lead them around with a leash.

I was still extremely frightened about meeting my maker, but I would much rather worry about my next adventure than worry about my final day. And as I continued to ponder these momentous thoughts, I somehow fell asleep with remarkable ease.

The next day, I stood outside waiting for Dan, Harold and James to come by. I wanted to show them the blueprints for the H.ID.J. It was a boat that I was planning on building for the summer. Of course, we would have to steal the wood from the construction site, which happened to be in the Jeep Man's territory.

And the HIDJ was only the start. We were going to have our best summer yet. We would hunt the mountain lion and the mysterious cave that were both rumored to be on the mountain. The Jeep Man, with a renewed vengeance, would be after our tails, and we would finally obtain our revenge against the wicked Dragon Lady.

It was peculiar. Perhaps the cure for death had been under my nose all along. Life, living it to its fullest, seemed to put death in its proper perspective. Or perhaps I would find the remedy later on. At the moment, I had bigger adventures ahead and for now, that was good enough for me.

THE END OF THE BEGINNING

Printed in the United States
2064